THE CHILDREN'S
HORRIBLE HOUSE

Eternal Spirit of the chainless Mind!
Brightest in dungeons, Liberty! thou art,
For there thy habitation is the heart—
The heart which love of thee alone can bind;

—Lord Byron
Sonnet on Chillon
1816

Love never fails, but it doesn't always
succeed. For love to be successful,
it must be received.
—Jeffrey R. Quackenbush

THE CHILDREN'S
HORRIBLE HOUSE

N. JANE QUACKENBUSH

For information regarding permission, write to:
Attention: Hidden Wolf Books
155 West Genung St., St. Augustine, FL 32086

Copyright © 2015 by N. Jane Quackenbush
All rights reserved.
Published in the United States by Hidden Wolf Books.

ISBN 9780991104567
LCN 2015954388

Text set in Adobe Garamond
Designed by Philip Benjamin

Version 1.2
Printed in the United States of America
First edition paperback printed, October 2015

*To my family: Mom and Dad, Jeffrey,
David, Jennifer, and Debbie*

Acknowledgments
*Special thanks to: Kika Iadanza for reading this book over
and over again and having special laser-beam eyes that
can spot errors; my mother, Virginia Quackenbush, also
for repeat readings and for finding the things Kika didn't;
my sons, Christian and Westly, for being so funny; Caitlyn
McCrea, for inserting those simple things I overlooked;
Christina Benjamin, for recognizing how weird I am and
loving it; Jaimie Engle, for content edits that made the
book so much better; and Phil Benjamin, for being a
bad-to-the-bone graphic designer.*

The Children's Horrible House

The chil - dren's hor - i - ble house--

The chil - dren's hor - i - ble house--

Where you work all day------

And nev - er nev - er play----

The chil - dren's hor - i - ble house!

This is the song that my older brothers and sisters used to sing to me when I didn't want to do my chores. Little did I know how serious they were, until one day when the bus for The Children's Horrible House came to pick me up ...

I'M HOLLY

CHAPTER 1
THE LETTER

"Holly," my mom called out, "time to make your bed."

Okay, see … there's something you should know. I never made my bed. So why was my mother telling me to?

"*GRRRR*," I groaned. I was too busy wondering what my older sister was talking about to her *boyfriend*. Yeah, her *boyfriend*. Isn't that so sickening? Yuck.

She was all, "Ooohh," and "Oh yeah? Uh-huh, oh, Basil, you're so funny."

Yuck, right?

I wrapped my arms around my shoulders, turned my back to her, and pretended to be kissing an imaginary something as I felt a pillow beam me in the back of my head. My ugly corrective glasses flew off my face.

"GO AWAY, you repugnant hemorrhoid." Ginger had a way of insulting me with words that were above my reading level, yet were understood clearly. I was no match to her wit.

Okay, okay, I thought as I bent down to pick up my glasses. I can take a hint. *Geez, Louise.*

"Mom," Ginger called, "tell your fifth child to leave me alone!"

"I *AM* leaving you alone, geez!" I left her room, looked into my messy room, and decided that I would rather go check out what my brother, Cashew, was doing. My fingertips brushed the flowery wallpaper as I skipped down the hallway and peeked into his room. He was making his bed. *Of course*, Cashew was making his bed. He had the smallest room in the whole house, but it was the neatest, with its quaint nautical theme. In the corner, a net filled with dried starfish and sand dollars was lit by a hanging lantern on a thick rope right above his bed which had a ship's steering wheel as the headboard.

"Hi, Cash … what are you doing?" I asked as I inspected his shell collection.

"I'm making my bed, same thing you should be doing."

As long as I could remember, my brother Cashew had always been naturally neat; he was also playful in a very convincing manner. "Or you'll be headed to … The Children's Horrible House." He sang that last part deep and slow.

A chill swept across my neck. "What's that?" I asked.

"What's what?" he asked.

"The Children's Horrible House."

"Oh, you mean," he started singing,

> *"The Children's Horrible House*
> *The Children's Horrible House*
> *Where you work all day and never, never play …*
> *The Children's Horrible House … ahhh!"*

I caught the slightest hint of his smile before he looked away.

"Is it even a real place? I've never heard it was real," I skeptically informed him.

Cashew sang a second verse:

> *"If you won't clean your room*
> *then you've sealed your doom.*
> *The Children's Horrible House ..."*

"I'm telling you now. You better go make your bed or you're going to find out when you go there," he said as he scooted me out of his room.

I didn't want to make my bed. I didn't want to make my bed at all. I have never had to make my bed before. My mom had suggested I make it plenty of times, but nothing ever happened before when I didn't do it.

Across the hall, I noticed that Ginger's bed was made. She sat at her vanity, clipping curlers in her hair. With the last one clipped in, her daily makeup routine commenced. But first, a careful inspection of the blank canvas that was her face was assessed. She was flaring her nostrils to see if she had any unwelcome boogers in her sniffer, when she noticed me in the reflection. Ginger gave me a nasty look, got up, and closed the door in my face.

I know, I thought. I can ask my sister, Juniper, to help me. She always helped me. She was the sister who kind of liked me. She would play with me in the dark attic and pretend to be a monster. We would be surrounded in blackness, then from behind my sister, I heard a rising, *"ROAR!"* I would squirm in her arms and she would hold and comfort me, saying in a soft, soothing voice, "It's okay, Holly. I'm here. I'll protect you!" As soon as it would get quiet again, I would hear a crackled *"ROAR!"* and I would cling to Juniper, scared all over again and she would once more come to my rescue.

Since Juniper was eight years older than I, she wasn't home as much as she used to be. She played the trumpet in the marching band, and she practiced daily. Black-and-white pictures of famous trumpet players decorated her walls. I noticed in her room, the musical printed covers were neatly tucked in on her bed, so I thought since she was finished making her bed, maybe she would help me make mine.

I didn't want to just ask her. I wanted to guarantee a "yes" from her. I thought about things I could do for her, so that in exchange she would do something for me. But I couldn't think of anything I could do for her.

I decided to use my recently acquired penmanship skills to craft a beautiful letter asking for her assistance in making my bed. I went back into my room and was digging around in the mess until I found my favorite lop-eared bunny hat. It always helped me think better and I would swing the ears back and forth, pretending that they were really my long, luxurious blonde hair.

After I carefully wrote the note, I looked it over and thought, WOW! That's a great-looking letter. I even drew a heart on it to sweeten the deal. I folded it up like a piece of origami and left a tag for her to tug, which would allow the letter to fall open like a treasure map. This was good, really good. I was sure she would appreciate the craftsmanship of this—not just letter—piece of art. I found her in my mom and dad's room talking to my mom about the band teacher. I ran in and handed her the note. I quickly dashed out, waiting for her response.

I imagined her opening the letter and being overcome by the beauty of my handwriting, appreciating each fold that made up this one-of-a-kind note. I imagined comforting her the same way she comforted me in the attic, that she would look into my eyes and nod, and say, "Of course I'll help my *widdle Holly Hocks*!"

I waited a while longer, but she didn't come out. I poked my head around the corner and noticed that she hadn't even opened the letter, much less been overcome by it. How could she resist such a fine-looking gift? I would have ripped that note open immediately if anyone cared enough to give me something so desirable. I wanted this to hurry along so I said in my most convincing voice, "June! I wrote you a letter. Are you going to read it?"

I must have interrupted something, because at first she just sat there; but then she slowly unfolded the letter, read it, and then started laughing. What was so funny? It was a simple request, not a joke or anything. She reread it and laughed harder this time. She got up and went into Cashew's room. She read him the letter out loud:

"DEAR JUNE,
   WILL YOU
          PLASE HAPPLE ME
MOCK MY BED?
   ♥ HOLLY"

Cashew seemed to think my letter was funny too. He was laughing and rereading the letter over and over, out loud as well.

Guess I was on my own. Guess I had to make my own bed and learn how to spell better. I walked back to my room and looked at my unmade bed. I looked at the mountain of sheets and blankets mixed with stuffed animals and socks. This would take forever. So I did what comes next when you don't want to do something: I complained.

"I'll never be able to make my bed! It's too hard! Plus, I'm just going to get back in it tonight and then I will have to make it all over again."

It didn't make any sense to me.

I guess they could hear me, because my brother called out and said, "You better make your bed before The Children's Horrible House comes to pick you up!"

"What's so horrible about the Children's Horrible House, anyway?" I grumbled.

"Well," my brother said, "at The Children's Horrible House, you have to make beds all day long, and as soon as you finish making every single bed, they come in and mess them up again! All day long, you make beds over and over and over …."

"That's not true!" I protested.

"Oh yes, it is," he insisted. "And Mom just called them, and they are on their way here to pick you up," Cashew said, trying to convince me with his half-kidding style.

I tried to not believe him, but something inside made me a little scared.

"Oh yeah. Mom? You called The Children's Horrible House to come pick up Holly?" Cashew called.

"Uh-huh!" said my mom's perpetually joyful voice.

Juniper and Cashew sang together:

> *"You better make your bed*
> *like your momma said."*

Juniper nonchalantly added, "Hey, Holl, don't worry. When they come to pick you up, they'll just keep you there a couple years or until you learn how to make beds the right way. You'll be okay, don't worry."

"June, can you call them to see if they're on their way?" I taunted, not believing them.

"Sure," Juniper said as she sauntered up to the phone. Little did I know, she was holding down the hangup button. "*Alloow*?" she said in an ultra professional British-sounding voice. "Is this The Children's Horrible House? Is it, now? Yes, thanks so much. … Yes, I am inquiring about the *shhheduled* pickup arrangements for one Holly *Spinooootsch*. Oh, dear. She simply refuses to make her bed and clean her room. So, it is true? Your coach is in transit? On its way, is it?" She widened her eyes at me in emphasis. "Oh dear, yes, yes, will do. Cheerio."

I couldn't help but get scared.

Juniper could do many accents … Southern, Northern, German, British, and even accents that she made up. I half thought she was joking, but she did her impersonations so believably that I almost thought she really was talking to The Children's Horrible House.

My eyes darted back and forth. I stood there, arrested in fear and disbelief, wondering if I should run away.

"It's okay, Holly. Maybe if you make your bed quickly and neat enough, they might not pick you up."

I ran up the stairs to my bedroom and looked at my messy bed. On it were piles of clothes, towels and stuffed animals. I could hardly make out the Holly Hobby wallpaper my mother so lovingly hung for me. But if my mom really loved me, why would she send me to The Children's Horrible House? I looked around my room and suddenly saw how messy it really was. I felt overwhelmed, so I called out, "What if I just pay them? Could I give them all my money and then they won't make me go?"

"Depends," said my oldest brother, Hickory, as he was walking upstairs, looking for my dad.

"Depends on what?" I asked.

"Depends on how much money you have," he sang in his usual deep tune of tones.

"Oh," I sprinted to my piggy bank, a big purple plastic poodle, hoping for big money. I picked it up and shook it. I could hear something inside. I took off the black rubber stopper and shook out the contents: four pennies, one nickel, a gum wrapper, gum in an already chewed wad, and some lint. I added it up and said, "Nine cents. Is that enough?"

"Hardly," my brother said with a not-so-funny chuckle. "Looks like you're headed to The Children's Horrible House." Then he groaned out some weird version of the song, mixed with his perpetual noisemaking.

My brother Hickory was an expert at making noise at all times. If he wasn't tunelessly humming, which sounded more like different inflections of "*Errrrrr, errrrrrrr, errrrrrrrr, errrrrrrrrr,*" he was burping out the alphabet or snoring. Hickory had two speeds: overdrive and comatose. He was a noisemaking daredevil while he was awake, but as soon as family movie time came, he would lie down on the floor with his one leg bent and his other foot resting on his knee, snoring away.

Throughout the house, upstairs and downstairs, I looked for more change. I dug in the couch cushions, opened all the junk drawers. After I counted it all up, I still had only seventy-eight cents. I pretty much knew that wouldn't be enough. Deflated, I went to my room and plopped on top of the stuff covering my bed. I turned to the only real friend I had, my hamster, Dookie. I looked into his glass cage and picked him up, got back on my bed, and placed him on my chest. He was so cute, with his "peanut butter and cream" fur, stumpy tail, and buttony black eyes. He twitched his nose for me as if he understood my plight. I thought maybe Dookie could come with me if I had to go to The Children's Horrible House. I could sneak him into my pocket! No, it was tight. Or, what if I ran away?

* * *

Deep within my subconsciousness, I heard the tune of The Children's Horrible House haunting my restlessness. I could hear the voices singing in low, frightening tones:

> *"You won't do your chore,*
> *now you're out the door.*
> *The Children's Horrible House ... ahhh!"*

My sister Juniper came into my room. With an urgent voice, she said, "Holly, they're here. You have to go with them. Come on, let's go. They're waiting for you." She grabbed my hands and pulled me off my bed.

"Who? Who's here waiting for me?" I asked as I slowly stood up.

"The Children's Horrible House bus is here! Now! They're here to pick you up." The fact that she wasn't using any funny accents alarmed me.

"But wait, I don't want to go. I promise I'll make my bed. Please, don't make me go!"

"It's too late, Holly. You should have made your bed when Mom asked you to make it. And now that they are here, there is nothing we can do to make them leave without you." She pulled me along and out of my room.

We walked by my mom and dad's room; they just sat there on the bed and looked down. They wouldn't look at me. I tried to call out, but my sister grabbed me and told me, "Stop. It's no use, Holly, you have to go. NOW!"

"But what about Dookie? Who is going with me?" I asked.

"No one. Everyone else cleaned their rooms and made their beds." She grabbed Dookie out of my cupped hands and ran back to put him in his cage.

When we came downstairs, I was shocked to see two dark men in white military-looking suits standing outside our front door. They stood in the driveway with their hands crossed in front of them. They were wearing sunglasses, so I couldn't see if they had kind eyes. It was like my brothers and sisters said it would be. They were in front of the big white bus. It had windows, but I couldn't see inside because there was dark tint on the windows and a sign on the side that read:

THE CHILDREN'S HORRIBLE HOUSE

in bold black letters that resembled the bars in a jail.

CHAPTER 2
THE MEN IN SUITS

"Be brave, Holly," Juniper said, "and do exactly what they tell you to do. The sooner you listen and learn, the sooner you can come home." She kissed the top of my head and walked me over to the men.

Without a word, the driver bowed down and then slid open the bus door to let me in. The chair was a bench with a seatbelt that I quickly fastened. I wanted to impress them with my safety precautions. Once inside, I was surprised that I could see out perfectly. The dark tint on the outside of the bus looked like stained-glass windows from the inside, although still perfectly translucent. It made everything outside look like it was colored in each hue of the rainbow.

I turned around to look at my house as we departed. Goodbye, Mom and Dad. … Goodbye, Hickory, Cashew, Juniper, and Ginger … goodbye, Dookie. Goodbye, house. My house never looked so charming as it did right then. Such a pretty white house with blue shutters now appeared purple with midnight shutters. It looked like the subject of a color-splashed farmhouse painting, so unassuming in its setting of rolling hills and towering trees in dotted patches surrounding the pond. While looking longingly at my house, I noticed another person in the back of the bus. It was a boy around my age. He had a purposeful look in his expression; I wasn't sure what it meant.

"Are you okay?" I asked.

His glass-green eyes focused on me from behind his dark side-swiped bangs. He skeptically nodded, but I wasn't convinced.

"What's your name? My name is Holly, and I guess you didn't make your bed or clean your room? Am I right?" I tried to lure him out of his shyness.

His eyes squinted at the corners and he said, "Maybe."

"'Cause I didn't make my bed either," I informed him.

I turned around and looked out the windshield to see where we were headed. The driver and the big brown muscular man looked as if this was going to be a long journey. I noticed a name tag on the visor above the muscle man. It looked like it was some sort of military identification; it had a photo which matched him and his name read: MAJOR WHOOPINS.

CHAPTER 3
THE MAN IN THE MOON

Major Whoopins, huh? ... Now, that's curious. I wondered what the bus driver's name was and then I realized I still didn't know the name of the boy behind me. I turned around and said, "You never told me your name."

"Coriander," he said so softly that I almost said, "Huh?" but then I figured out what he had said.

"Hi, Coriander, I'm Holly. Have you ever been to where we are going?"

"No," he answered.

"Oh. Well, do you know anything about where it is that we are going?"

"Ummm." He hesitated and then said, "No, not really."

"Okay." I realized for the first time in my life, I was on my own.

We drove and drove, even into the night. The soft tune of "The Children's Horrible House," the song my brothers and sisters had been singing to me all day, quietly streamed from the van speakers. The moon shone strongly through the front passenger side window. I could see that it was following us. Seeing the moon made me feel a little better. I imagined the man on the moon settling down in his rocking chair next to a fire he lit, so warm and so comforting, we all could see its glow. He was probably sipping on some hot cocoa while he enjoyed the warmth of his hearth. I visualized myself there as I drifted off to sleep.

I was jolted awake by the quick stop of the bus and the loud puff of air let out by the brakes, followed by the engine grumbling about being turned off.

"Everybody up and out," Major Whoopins called.

I immediately climbed out of the van, hoping to once again impress them with my obedience. *Where are we?* My glasses had shifted off to the side, so I put them back on straight. I looked at the very large spooky building and noticed a sign that read: The Children's Horrible House. There was no question as to where I was. My brothers and sisters were right. They said if I didn't make my bed and clean my room that I would go to The Children's Horrible House … and here I was.

I wish I would have listened.

CHAPTER 4
THE FLAMING GATE

It was still dark when we were let out in front of a huge flaming gate. Well, the gate wasn't actually flaming, but on each side, a gas lantern was lit and with the smudges on my eternally foggy glasses, it made the gate appear ablaze. The shiny black metal not only reflected the flames, but it seemed to make the whole gate glow in unison with the flickering flames. A very tall brick wall covered in thorny bushes grew even higher than the wall, spreading out of sight in both directions. Major Whoopins punched in a code that opened the gates.

We proceeded down a long black driveway lined with spooky cowering trees offering a creepy welcome. Ahead I saw a building. Even though it was still not quite morning, the sun had started to peek over the horizon, giving us just the right light to see. It was a three-story, maroon-colored mansion that looked like it could either be a haunted Victorian house or the fanciest jail ever constructed. I wasn't sure. It looked like a jail because it had bars on the windows, but it also looked like a fancy house because it had white painted porches on the first two stories. The roof line was very steep and had a couple of chimney stacks. The front right side of the building had a square turret that made it look nice, but frightening. At the top of the turret, I noticed a bar-less window with lace curtains. As I stared, I felt someone staring back. A woman's form moved from behind the curtain, and then she was gone.

"Who was that?" I asked, mostly to myself, but I guess Major Whoopins heard me because he answered me, saying in a thick, gruff voice, "You'd best mind yo' own bidness and you gonna git along just fine, ya' hear?"

"Yes, sir!" I said hoping to stay on his good side. He gave me a reluctant smile, but I saw it.

"See that door?" he asked. "You go on and git up there and wait fo' Mr. Ree."

Who was Mr. Ree? I wondered.

I pushed my glasses back up my nose and walked to the door. Just to the right of the enormous door was a hanging cylindrical cage. There was a group of weary kids sitting inside waiting for their release.

"Hey, you! Hey!" they called out to me as I continued toward the entrance. It was the biggest solid wooden door that I had ever seen; it must have been hundreds of years old. It had carvings of a farmer steering oxen to plow a field. Big iron straps ran horizontally across the front, and at the top shimmered stained glass. Below the glass hung a big round door knocker. It was made of iron and looked very heavy. I reached up to see what would happen if I lifted it and knocked on the door.

Just when I had the ring in my hand, one of the kids in the cage yelled out, "Help us!" from behind and startled me. I dropped the ring, with a loud thunk so loud that it thunked again. And that startled me even more! I turned around as I was whisked inside the huge building.

Turns out, Mr. Ree was the bus driver. He held my hand in the not so fun, holding hand kind of way, while ushering me in and around the enormous building. It seemed so very big, but that could have been because I am very small in comparison, though not small compared to my friends. I actually come from a very tall family although, sadly, I have never been cute. I am probably on the ugly side, considering that most girls confused me for being a boy, yet boys, most certainly knew that I was not a boy. The thick corrective glasses I wore didn't add to my looks much, either. They made my eyes look magnified.

I hated my glasses, but since I had a little crush on my eye doctor—who looked like Clark Kent, who was actually Superman—I continued to wear the awful things; plus, I could see a lot better.

As I was being ushered around, I noticed a plaque on the wall with a sign on it that read:

At first it didn't register. I simply read the letters and phonetically put them together to form the name. But then it dawned on me ... Sirius Pankins ... Spankins ... that doesn't seem very promising. You mean to tell me the director of The Children's Horrible House's name was Sirius Pankins?

I knew all about spankings. My dad was the spank master. He had even carved out a special paddle for when my brothers, sisters, and I needed a reminder to be good. Even though my sister Ginger didn't think I was very intelligent, I was smart enough to hide the paddle. Good thing; for the most part, he didn't have to use it. When he demanded to know where it was, it had been hiding for so long that I didn't remember where I had put it ... so I wasn't lying when I said I didn't know where it was.

Mr. Ree knocked on the door to the office and we went inside. A lady sat behind a desk, busily typing. Her hands seemed to dance across the keyboard. At some points, her fingertips would leap off each letter like they were in a ballet and at the end of each line she would usher the carriage return bar over to the beginning with such dramatic flair that was quite opposite of the rest of her body language, which was sedate. The nameplate on her desk read: MISS TAKE, OFFICE ADMINISTRATOR.

Mr. Ree waited for her to look up; then he bowed. I guess that was something normal to his culture. I bowed too, thinking it was a nice gesture. Her eyes glanced up but the rest of her face pointed down as her glasses pinched firmly above the lower part of her nose. Her nostrils flared perfectly, acting as tiny platforms to keep her lenses from descending further.

"Name?" she asked.

"Holly Spinatsch."

"Spell that, please."

As I spoke each letter, her fingers slowly and elegantly glided to each key.

"Penalty?" she asked Mr. Ree.

"Not making her bed or cleaning her room." Her fingers tap-danced double-time.

"Punishment?"

"Making beds and cleaning rooms, among other things. But we will see."

Her hands recorded my crimes and punishment with such animated gusto that I couldn't stop my smile from forming, but not for long. She shook her head in dismay and showed her disappointment by clicking her tongue.

"You know where to take her, Mr. Ree," she said.

"Sure do, Miss Take. See you in a bit with the next one." He bowed again as we left. I did the same as I wondered who would be next.

CHAPTER 5

Many Years Prior at

The North Star Estate

It wasn't my fault that I turned out like this, Saffron brooded. *How would you act if your mother left you at eight years old?* Saffron didn't have a clear interpretation of her identity. She had a sense who people would like her to be, but being that person was not interesting to her. She knew that she was born in the middle of the Perseid meteor shower that occurs in August. Her father would tell her this as if it should mean something. At the time, Saffron offered little to let her father know she cared. When he didn't know what else to do, he would give her things so she would go away, or so she thought. "I'll go away," she promised.

She often overheard the household staff talk about her older half-brothers and half-sisters and how much better they all were compared to her. Their mother, Hyacinth, died giving birth to her last child. The older kids went away to boarding school and the baby girl went to live with her grandparents. Saffron met them only once, right before her mother, Sings-in-the-Meadow, went missing.

Saffron's father, Hawthorne North Star, was a widower when he met Sings-in-the-Meadow. Saffron's mother was very different from Hyacinth, based on the portraits she had seen. Saffron loved and missed her mother terribly. She couldn't figure out why her mother would leave her. She was pretty sure, at the time her mom left, she hadn't been so bad.

Sings-in-the-Meadow was Native American, with long, black, blanketing hair. She would cover Saffron in it like a teepee. Her smiling face would be illuminated at the top, like the sun. Saffron remembered her mouth moving in a language her ears couldn't understand, but somehow her mind knew the meanings. When her mother went away, the part of Saffron that was able to love went with her and she was left with an empty, callous shell free of all emotions … except bitterness.

CHAPTER 6

Present Time at
THE CHILDREN'S HORRIBLE HOUSE

"Did you say somethin', Miss Pankins?" Major Whoopins asked as she was calculating the course of this month's lunar cycle.

She was unaware of her murmuring as she looked up from her guide. "No, did you?"

"Yes, I mean, no …." He shook his head, but decided to just continue. "Yo' new pupils have arrived. Should I show them in to tha' ballroom?"

Director Pankins straightened up in her seat and silently made preparations as she arose. Major Whoopins held open her jacket as she circled her way inside. She pulled up her white collar to look most severe. "Yes, show them in," she said in her deep, evocative voice.

Major Whoopins hesitated as he zeroed in on her mouth.

Did you want to wipe off yo' mouth firs'? He wanted to say, but he was too intimidated by her radiating, flame-like eyes. Major Whoopins was not used to feeling powerless, but somehow Director Pankins could summon this uncomfortable feeling from anyone.

"Is there a problem?" she questioned, annoyed at his staring. She squinted her malevolent eyes at him, willing him to continue to make eye contact. There was not a soul alive who could win a staring contest against Sirius Pankins. It was like staring into the sun.

"Oh, it's nothin'." He *now* pretended not to notice as he whistled nonchalantly.

＊　＊　＊

Mr. Ree and I exited the office and continued down the corridor until we entered a large gymnasium-sized room. It had to be the fanciest gym I had ever seen, with its large crystal chandeliers hanging from the silk-pleated ceilings. The hardwood floors spread in a zigzag pattern. A metal grid in diamond shapes decorated the tall windows and long curtain panels flanked each side.

Rows of other kids lined up in specific groups. At the front of each line there was a cursive letter placed on a post, and from the left side of the room, the letters continued alphabetically. I was taken to the letter *S*. Needless to say, the line was long with other naughty kids, and I stood at the back of the line.

Everyone was waiting, when suddenly we heard a loud and soft thump followed by loud, bass-filled organ music. It was deep and thunderous and ended with a clanging of large cymbals. Everyone fell silent and covered their ears.

The double doors opened and a procession of uniformed men and women began to come through. They marched, holding up flags, with Major Whoopins leading the group. The flags had a rendering of The Children's Horrible House with the initials in script at the bottom. It looked creepy yet really cool. I was so fascinated by all the pomp and circumstance.

At the center of the room was a podium. Behind it, a well-dressed woman stood waiting for the appropriate time to speak. She cleared her throat.

"Eh-hem, excuse me, children," she said directly in a very strong but not loud voice. "My name is Director Sirius Pankins, and you may all address me as such. You have all come here from different places, from different families, but you are all here for the same reason ... your disobedience. You are here because of you. You will be here as long as you are disobedient. When you have learned true obedience, and I mean true obedience, you may return home. If you fail to learn, you will be taken from this facility to another undisclosed facility where, let me tell you, you will learn the hard way. And you will wish your obedience was not an option, that you were a robot with no aptitude for selfish motivations."

She outlined what we could expect from our stay, and it seemed my brothers and sisters knew more than I thought. After she finished speaking, she stepped out from behind the podium and walked around the room, eyeing a child here and there. The room silenced except for the deliberate tic and tac of her footfalls. She made her way to the back of the room and was walking in my general direction—closer, closer, and closer—until she stopped right beside me. At first, she just stood there like she had no purpose. Then she turned directly to me and lifted one of the long ears from my bunny hat and twirled it around in her fingers while staring into my eyes. I kept my eyes focused on the wall in front of me, not meeting hers directly. She asked for my name.

"Holly Sp-Sp-Spinatsch, ma'am."

"Sp-Sp-Spinatsch?" she repeated. I heard a collective giggle. "Wow, that's one I've never heard before!" She smiled as she discarded my bunny ear.

As you may have figured out, yes, everyone laughed. And yes, they were laughing *at* me, not *with* me. But the thing is, since I was born with this name, Spinatsch, everyone has always laughed at me, so this was really nothing new. I was used to people making fun of my name in front or behind my back. They would try to be funny by calling me "Spinach Breath" or "Holly Spinach Quiche," but I guess since it was already as quirky as it could get, all the other not-so-funny names got old … and people moved on. As weird as it sounds, my last name was probably the most normal thing about me.

Director Pankins was hoping to make an example out of me, which is why she looked around with a huge grin spread across her mouth, which happened to expose some food in between her front teeth. Ironically, it looked like spinach. I inadvertently must have made a face, with my tongue trying to grab phantom spinach from between my front teeth. Director Pankins noticed. She stopped, mimicked my gesture, and tried to pry it out with her fingernail; finally, she pulled out a compact mirror, bared her teeth, and quickly plucked the glob out from between her teeth. "Eh-hem." She narrowed her eyes at me and moved on.

Phew … I felt my trapped breath exhale in relief. But before I knew it, she quickly looked back at me with a gnarled face, promising that trouble was soon to be upon me.

CHAPTER 7
FIRE ANTS

After our assembly, we were ushered to our rooms. We were each assigned a bunk and a uniform. The room was long and skinny, with a window with scrolled iron bars on it at the far end. I was issued a bottom bunk, which made me happy and scared. What if the person on top was really heavy and they fell on me? On the other hand, it could be like a full-time blanket fort. I had a tendency to want to build them out of blankets and pillows in my living room back home. I also loved building them out of big appliance boxes, but I had to do that kind of construction outside.

Not long ago, I was putting some finishing touches on one of my big box fort masterpieces, when something started to bite me. I was working away, sitting down in the dirt with my legs crisscrossed, and suddenly I was being bitten all over my body. I was covered in fire ants. I screamed! I tried to wipe them off, but they still bit me. I started to panic, but then my dad came around and picked me up by my underarms with my legs still crossed.

He said, "You're sitting in an ant pile!"

I looked down and saw a frenzy of ants going in every direction. My mom came out, took me, and set me down. She brushed off the remaining ants and put me in a bath. Moms always know what to do.

Blanket forts were safer—I never had anything bad happen to me in any of my inside blanket forts, so I felt pretty safe here with my new bunk accommodations.

By the looks of this bed, I felt extra good. It looked so well made, so deliberate in all its tucks. With the top sheet folded so neatly over the fluffy blanket, it looked like someone had used a ruler to get each side exactly right. The top sheet and blankets were turned down on just one side. A decorative pillow placed in the very center of the bed gave it the right adorning touch. The small squishy pillow must have been filled with the softest stuffing possible. I picked it up and held it to my face. It smelled like lavender flowers and warm breezes. Not only beautiful, but this bed offered supreme comfort. I pushed on the mattress, feeling its soft yet firm support. This is probably what my mom was going for when she asked me to make my bed and clean my room. There wasn't a stitch out of place. I have to admit, it made me feel better. As I was admiring my new sleeping situation, two girls walked up to my bed and plopped down, messing up all the beautifully made covers and pillows.

"Nice bed, huh! Well, it's mine, thaaaanks …" one said dismissively as she threw the throw pillow in my face. I wished I was ready for that, but it caught me right in the center of my face, causing my glasses to fall off one ear and what hair I had exposed to fluff back in response.

"But, I thought this was mine. I was issued a bottom bunk," I insisted while straightening my glasses.

They mimicked me: *"But this is my bed, I was issued a bottom bunk,"* they said in hysterics. "You *were* issued a bottom bunk; it's right over *there*." They pointed to the bed at the end of the room near the window. The room seemed to grow longer as my eyes looked for the indicated bed. I found the heap and my once comforting thoughts of sweet slumber disappeared in a poof. As I walked, I heard them snickering about me and my horrible-looking bed. When I got to it, it was a pile of who knows what. It resembled the unmade bed I had left in my room at home.

We were told to put on our plain uniforms. I was used to my corduroy cutoffs and Oscar the Grouch T-shirt, if I was wearing a shirt at all. I preferred to dress like my older brothers, not all nice and frilly in dresses like my sisters. Dresses are for girls. And I was a tomboy who happened to like a long-eared bunny hat that I had to remove in order to get dressed. The uniform was a white coverall, so it was fine with me … just so long as it wasn't a dress.

As I was getting dressed, I heard some shrieks. I looked around and since I had just taken off my hat and my glasses, everything was fuzzy, but I still saw the other girls all looking and pointing at me. They had looks of horror as well as a few grimaces. One of the girls who had the courage to speak for the rest said, "You're a boy! You're not supposed to be in here. This is a girls' room!"

Some of the other girls ran out and called for help from the dorm monitor.

"I'm not a boy," I said as I buttoned up the coverall.

"Could'a fooled me," I heard another one of them say.

They all stared and that made me feel uncomfortable, so I turned away. As I turned, I saw that Cassia, one of the girls who had run out, had retrieved an adult, Miss Fitz. Cassia was leading Miss Fitz, pleading with her, "Please, Miss Fitz, get this boy out of the girls' room!"

I started to panic. I ran for the bathroom and held the door closed so no one could come in and get me. At first I didn't see the other girls in the restroom who now looked scared. I guess they thought I was a boy, too.

"Hey, you get out of here right this minute," Miss Fitz called.

I didn't know what to do. I was stuck. The girls in the restroom started to scream. I must have let go of the door, because Miss Fitz came crashing in. I felt a flurry of hands banging all around my head. Then she grabbed me by an arm and led me away. I tried to explain, but she pushed me out the door, and before I knew it she was taking me to the director's office.

Phooey.

I hadn't even been here twenty-four hours and I was already in trouble. I walked into the office and went past Miss Take's desk. She greeted me with disappointment, which was not a hard look for her to achieve with her glasses so low on her nose. I was placed in front of Director Pankins' desk. I looked at the nameplate again and noticed the *S* in front of Pankins and wondered what it stood for. Was it Severe or Sinister? Then I remembered … it was Sirius.

CHAPTER 8
I'M NOT A BOY

She was seated in a tall-backed leather chair. Her arms draped the chair like she was seated for a portrait. But the look she reserved for me was not very becoming. It was a look of pure disgust. Behind her was a painting of a beautiful woman who looked to be Native American. She was holding a little girl. They were in the middle of a meadow surrounded by woods and flowers. It was a very pretty painting. I was lost in it until Director Pankins' scolding voice interrupted my meanderings.

"How dare you! A boy in the girls' dorm *and* bathroom ... well, this is a first. Do you know what I'm going to do? *DO YOU KNOW WHAT I'M GOING TO DO?*" she repeated louder.

I had no idea what she was going to do, but I was pretty sure it involved a paddle and my butt. I looked around her office trying to find the paddle my butt might encounter. She got up from her chair and came around her desk, but before she got to me, she stopped in front of a huge telescope. As she looked through the lens, her weight shifted around; she seemed to find something of importance. It must not have been what she was looking for because she quickly reset her stern gaze on me as she walked over to stand directly in front of me. I didn't get the chance to put on my glasses and without them, I looked extra boyish. My butt started to anticipate the beating. It was clenching so hard that I got a butt cramp.

"You. … What is your name?"

"Holly Sp-Sp-Spinatsch, ma'am," I replied.

Her face morphed into a confused predator as she tried to make sense of the boy in her office with a name like Holly Spinatsch.

"That is strange. … I've heard that name before … not too long ago, I think. … Oh, yes, yes, I remember you, but why would you have a name like Holly? Did your parents want a girl or something? Wait a second. Didn't you look different before?" She cleared her throat, looked away, adjusted her face, and then looked directly at me.

"Are you a boy?" she asked.

"No, I'm a girl … ma'am."

"Well, why do you look like a boy?" she demanded.

I shrugged.

"Are you sure? You are a girl?"

"I'm sure. My mom cuts my hair real short 'cause I don't clean it very much and without my bunny hat and glasses, this is what I look like."

Most other girls would be crying by now, but nope, not me. I was tough. It would take a lot more than this to get me to cry.

"Your bunny hat and glasses," she muttered, and cleared her throat.

"I see. … Well, I don't have the time to deal with such nonsense. You will have to return to your room and I will inform Miss Fitz of your correct gender." She walked toward the door. As she stood there holding the door, she told me, "I better not see you in my office again."

Up close, I could see her interesting Dijon mustard–colored eyes. They stood out against her copper skin and toasted dark hair. Her lips sneered apart as she drilled her invective eyes into mine, revealing red lipstick on her teeth. It made her look like she was a vampire who just finished sucking life from her victim. I lifted my fingers to wipe my teeth. She closed her mouth suddenly. Her eyes narrowed as I walked out. When I looked behind me, I saw her staring at herself in her compact mirror, rubbing off the lipstick. As she did, her eyes began to slide out from behind the mirror, but before they made it, I turned around quickly and walked toward my room. I could feel her narrowed eyes piercing my short-haired head.

✳ ✳ ✳

When I got to the door, I was reluctant to go inside. I was so sure everyone was going to gang up on me. I must have really good instincts, because that is exactly what happened.

"Hey, boy, I thought we told you to leave. This is our room, the girls' room," Nettle, the girl who stole my pretty bed earlier, informed me.

I thought it was funny because she kind of had a boy's haircut too. Her hair was short in the front like mine, but her hair was long in the back. I guess that was the style. She had dark hair, brown slit-like eyes and dark skin. Her friend and back-up partner, Thistle, had black, shoulder-length, wavy hair and buck teeth, which may or may not have been the cause of her prominent lisp. Her teeth looked bent in, trying unsuccessfully to stop her loud mouth from being a jerk.

"Yeah, thisth is the girls'th room," bucktooth Thistle said.

"I know that; I am a girl," I tried to explain.

"You don't look like one."

"Well, I am one." I started to walk to my bunk.

Great. Looks like they want to follow me. I sat down and put on my glasses. They stood right in front of me. I was hoping this would make them see that I was a girl.

"What are you, gay or thomething? Becauth you look like a boy."

I kind of knew what she meant by her tone, but when I was younger, my sister Juniper told me that being gay meant you had holes in your socks. I looked down at my socks and noticed the little holes in them and curled my toes trying to hide my gayness. I couldn't help that my socks had holes in them.

I looked at their socks and noticed that they had a few holes in their socks too, and my eyes began to squint at their hypocrisy. But I was scared to bring this obvious oversight to their attention. I didn't really know how I should respond. So I just looked at them and then down at their socks, trying to hint at their holes.

"Ew, she is gay! Look, she's staring at us!"

Thankfully, this made them leave … for a bit.

CHAPTER 9
MAKE FRIENDS

Miss Fitz came in and told us that it was time for our physicals. One by one we were examined to make sure we were fit for work. Some of the kids tried to act as if they were not capable, but I guess the staff knew the false signs to look for because everyone passed. Even the kid with one leg longer than the other, as well as the kid with the wiggly back were fit for work. Eventually it was my turn.

"Holly *Spinaaatsch*," the nurse, Miss Treetment, called in a manner that made her sound already fed up with me. To say that she looked tired was an incredible understatement. She looked like she had never slept in her life. The bags under her eyes were packed for going on a six-month-long vacation. The skin tags that dotted the puffy area below her eyes were magnified by her impossibly thick glasses, which had to weigh ten pounds. I scrunched my nose and thought how glad I was that mine weren't as thick or heavy. Good thing she had a strong nose and a cord to hold them around her neck, in case they fell.

She was holding a chart. She took my temperature, and then measured my height and weight. She had me bend over to check my spine. She did a hearing test and an eye exam.

"Child, you have the eyesight of an eighty-year-old granny," she informed me.

My eye doctor had told me the same thing. She recorded my height and asked me, "Where did you get your height from? You're tall for your age."

I thought about it, and my brother, Hickory, was the tallest member of our family at six foot four inches, and I answered her, "My brother." She let out a single laugh. "Okay." She shrugged. Lastly, she combed through my hair, looking for lice. It felt good to be groomed even if it was mandatory. Guess I checked out because I was sent to the dining hall.

The dining hall was huge, with large stained-glass windows. There were round chandeliers with lightbulbs that seemed to flicker like flames. They were flames, I realized, as I looked closer. The tables were square and seated four, but some larger groups pushed a couple tables together to accommodate themselves. The wooden chairs had very high carved backs. At my school cafeteria, we sat at long ugly picnic tables. Here, it was like a five-star hotel. On the rich wood-paneled walls were paintings of important-looking people. They were dressed in old-fashioned fancy clothes and seated in lavish, aureate chairs. The biggest painting hung above the gigantic fireplace. It was in the center of the side wall. It was of a handsome man with white hair and a white mustache. Below the painting hung a plaque that read: **Hawthorne North Star – Founder Of The Hawthorne House For Children.**

I repeated his title in my head and was confused. I thought I was at The Children's Horrible House. Maybe they wrote that wrong or perhaps the name had been changed, but why would it be changed to something that sounded so … *horrible*? I wondered.

I walked to the food line, surprised to find that even though this place was elaborate and fancy, it still had lunch ladies. They wore hair nets on their heads, rubber gloves, and they slopped the food on plates like we were prisoners. Miss Shapen was the head lunch lady. Her full-figured body sloshed in rhythm like one big set of water balloons as she walked around keeping a close eye on food consumption.

When I had my tray of food, I realized I had to find a seat. I walked slowly toward the girls' table, but when I saw the two girls who thought I was a boy, Thistle and Nettle, they made it very clear that I was not to sit with them.

Next to the enormous fireplace, I found a table with just one boy eating his food. I weaved through the other tables just as another boy, who happened to look exactly like the first boy, sat down beside him. I did a double take wondering if I should still assert myself, and then I just went for it. I sat down with the twins. All of my hesitation was for nothing because they hardly noticed. It was fine with me because I really wanted to eat and not talk.

Sounds easy, right? No, the food wasn't what I would call gourmet. My plate was cold ham chunks, quartered brown apples, and wilted lettuce cheese wraps. I looked up at the warm fireplace trying to swallow the hardly edible victuals and noticed an oval wooden plaque beneath the mantle, which read:

Whatever good thing
each one does,
This he will receive back.

The twins followed my gaze as I noticed their apparent cowlicks. They gave me a little snicker as they ate this foul meal.

"So," I said, "this is gross ..." as my ham cubes thunked the tray after I let them drop.

I guess they thought I was funny because they both laughed, and not *at* me. When they laughed, I could see their dimples, which were interesting; they were in the exact same spot, but on opposite cheeks, like their cowlicks. It was as if their faces had been perfectly stuck together, face to face, and when they were pulled apart their dimples and cowlicks were the evidence left behind. They were mirror images of each other and had very kind freckled faces, especially when they smiled.

"What are your names?" I asked.

"I'm Staniel, he's Danley," the slightly bigger twin informed me in his scratchy, crackled voice.

My brows slammed together like two polar magnets. I must have heard him wrong.

"You mean, Daniel and Stanley?" I asked.

"Nope," they replied in a single passive voice.

"Okay," I agreed. "Nice to meet you, Staniel and Danley."

"You too, Spinach." They laughed in their endearing, raspy voices.

I guess when you have a last name like mine, you can't judge those with questionable first names ... so we were in this together. I smiled and tried to eat my food. I left a lot behind even though I was super hungry.

* * *

A chime went off, indicating the end of mealtime. Everyone got up, cleared their trays, and were instructed to go back to the dorm room and wait for further instructions.

When I got back to my room, a girl was sitting on my unmade bed. She made no attempt to get up when I came in. She looked at me and I looked at her. Great, I thought ... more drama.

But she got up. As she walked away, she said, "I know you."

CHAPTER 10
THE FART

"Huh?" I wondered. *"How?"* I followed her into the hallway and asked. But she continued walking away.

That was weird, I thought. How does she know me? I don't think I know her. More girls started to walk toward the dorm room. As they did, I noticed these two girls who were yapping away like two Chihuahuas. It made me jealous. I wished that I had a best friend here. I felt really lonely. The two girls were going on and on. The one girl had a deep voice for a girl, and a funny accent. It reminded me of one of the many accents my sister, Juniper, would imitate. She was talking about her dogs, but when she said dog, she said, *"DAWWG."* All the other words sounded funny, too.

We were told to assemble into a line at the door. The two girls were behind me. I waited for her to say, *"DAWWG"* again. When she finally did say it, I started to laugh. They got quiet when I laughed. I turned to her and asked her to say dog again.

"Why?" she asked with hesitation.

"I like the way you say it," I told her.

"DAWWG?" she asked.

I laughed again. She and her friend laughed too. I felt relief, because she looked a little tough. She had blonde hair and very blue eyes. A scattering of moles on her face looked like the beginning of a constellation.

"What's your name?" I asked.

"Clova," she replied as she blinked like the genie in the old sitcom, *I Dream of Jeannie.*

"Clova?" I asked, wondering why she continued blinking. "How do you spell that?"

"C-L-O-V-E-R," she spelled slowly.

"Oh, Clover!" I stated.

"Yeah, Clova," she agreed, and blinked again.

Miss Fitz led us into a big theater. It was opulent, to say the least. For a place that was named "Horrible," it was actually magnificent. The windowless room wasn't huge; it was quite cozy. It was decorated in gold and scarlet. The carpeting was the most beautiful shade of red, with golden swirls that formed medallions. The walls were covered in detailed paintings of people dancing in a beautiful, rich setting. The stage was centered in the front with heavy purple velvet curtains lined with gold fringe. They draped in luxury, flanking the stage like a royal robe.

We were led to the front and then told to sit systematically in the rows of thick upholstered folding chairs. After we were all seated, the cascading curtains opened and a screen dropped. The movie began. It was in black and white except for Director Pankins' bright red lips, which seemed to reach out from the screen like they were in 3-D.

"Welcome, children, I am Director Sirius Pankins. You are here because you have been naughty, bratty, or otherwise disobedient.

During your time here at The Children's Horrible House, you will be reformed from your despicable, abhor-able, behavior. Now, if possible, please enjoy the following movie on how to properly make beds and clean rooms."

The movie began. I could hear the projector ticking away as it performed its sole purpose. The music as well as the images were, let's just say, poor quality and it wasn't what anyone would call exciting. I tuned out at about this time; I was sure it was all the same stuff. I started to get restless and I guess I wasn't the only one, because suddenly everyone was closing their noses and holding their breath. They were waving their hands around like something smelled. Then it hit me. A stink bomb blew up my nostrils and filled them with the most disgusting fart smell ever. Rotten eggs, decomposing sewage mixed with skunk were the images that came to mind as the cloud enveloped the theater. I felt hot as panic began to set in.

Everyone got up and charged for the door, but Mr. Meanor, one of Director Pankins' mean old enforcers, blocked us from escaping. When the smell invaded his nasal cavity, like an army of smelly soldiers, he couldn't take it anymore and he opened the door, gasping for fresh air. Everyone charged the door and left the room except for me. I didn't know where to go, and I did not want to be sent to Director Pankins' office again, so I waited for someone to tell me where I should go. I wondered who did it. Who farted so offensively? The odor began to dissipate as I was waiting, when Thistle and Nettle walked in.

"Ew! Oh my gosh, you are tho gross. You farted!" Thistle yelled, and they ran out the door.

Clover walked in and asked, "Was that you? Was that your fart?"

"NO! Someone else farted and then everyone left the room, but

I didn't know where to go, so I stayed. And now the room stinks and I guess since I'm the only one in here, they thought it was me, but it wasn't me."

"Why did you stay here?"

"I was afraid I would get in more trouble." I was getting upset now. It wasn't quite a cry, but it was serious embarrassment. I couldn't wait for this day to be over.

Mean old Mr. Meanor came back in, used his bulbous nose to sniff around, making sure the stench had dissipated, and then corralled us to our rooms for the rest of the night.

I stood before my messy bed and pulled everything off. I sifted through the pile and found the mattress topper and the foam pad and placed them on the top. I secured the bottom fitted sheet and then put on the top sheet. I looked back at the other beds for example and placed the coverlet on top.

I remembered my first sleepover at my grandparents' home and how they made the bed for me. It made me feel special. I had this amazing dream too, where I flew around on my bed through outer space. I turned down my coverlet and sheets just like my grandparents had done for me. I felt a bit better as I tucked myself into my freshly made bed.

I still worried about my erroneous smelly reputation. I wondered if that fart would haunt my entire existence here.

CHAPTER 11

Many Moons Ago at

The North Star Estate

I hate it here. I hate this house. I hate the staff. I hate their families and I hate my dad. Saffron silently fumed. Her dad always had this concerned expression on his old face. She wanted to leave. She decided it was time. She was fifteen and a half years old and her father still treated her like she was a toddler, offering her childish dolls, stuffed animals, and diaries.

When Saffron was a child, her father had turned the entire attic into a giant playroom. When her mother was still home, she would play in there for hours. Saffron used to play dress-up in her mother's native clothing. She would hop around in black dyed moccasins, doing her best native dance impressions. Her father, Hawthorne North Star, had a miniature mansion made, a replica of their house. It was filled with ornate furniture and lifelike dolls. When she played with her dollhouse, the Native American influence faded from focus and Saffron would transform in an instant into the role of her father's lineage.

Along the walls were shelves lined with every toy imaginable, even a special doll dressed in deerskins and black moccasins that looked remarkably like her mother. This magical place where she could let her imagination roam freely was Saffron's sanctuary, but when her mother, Sings-in-the-Meadow left, she felt so lonesome that not even the fantasy world that came alive in the attic would keep Saffron from missing her.

* * *

Saffron wanted to see what was on the other side of the tall brick walls which surrounded The North Star Estate. She had had brief experiences on the outside, but never on her own. Her father sent her to boarding school like he had done with his other children, but Saffron would get expelled or run away.

She walked into his study, also known as the library, where he was writing things down in a giant leather-bound book. He owned thousands of books and they were all carefully arranged and displayed for any scholar's reading pleasure. He loved being surrounded by all this sophisticated wisdom; whereas Saffron had absolutely no interest in reading his books. They all looked incredibly big and boring.

He looked up at Saffron with his disturbed face. He exhaled and shook his head. It was like he was disappointed or something. He seemed apprehensive, but he worked up enough courage to speak.

"I've just finished talking with a few members of our staff, Saffron, and they are not very happy with you. Apparently, you have been misbehaving and treating them in a most unbecoming manner. Is this true?" he asked, hoping that what he had heard was false.

Saffron knew it was true, but she couldn't care less about what the staff thought. She shrugged in obstinance.

"I'm sorry, Daddy. It won't happen again; I promise." These words were her fallback and they always worked, so she used them over and over. It was like this every time. He would look deep into her eyes, exploring her desolate, angered soul, hoping for some vestige of his beloved Sings-in-the-Meadow. Saffron realized she had to change her tactic if she was going to get her way.

CHAPTER 12
THE CHILDREN'S HORRIBLE HOUSE
MAKING BEDS AGAIN AND AGAIN

I was lying in my bed, thinking about the day, questioning myself if I would ever fall asleep. A light rain was falling outside, which usually lulled me to sleep. I looked around and watched a girl in the next bunk as she sucked her thumb. Wasn't she too old for thumb-sucking? As she was rhythmically calming herself, she used her index finger to caress her nose. She seemed very comforted by this motion. I had stopped sucking my thumb years ago! I gloated to myself on my maturity.

I remember my father coming in to put me to bed. He saw me soothing myself, with my thumb firmly placed inside my mouth, while my pinky stood straight up, like a flag on a mailbox. My dad took my free hand in his, looked me in the eye, and said, "Holly, how old are you?"

I blinked because I was pretty sure he knew how old I was, but I answered him even while my thumb still sat in my mouth. "I'm five."

"That's right," he agreed. "You are now five years old; no more sucking your thumb!"

I popped my thumb out and never sucked it again. I don't know how he did it, but it worked.

I started to miss my mom and dad. Usually, my mom would read me a story from *The Chronicles of Narnia* and tuck me into bed. Story time with my mother was something I really enjoyed. My bedtime was 8:00 p.m., and most of the time I resisted this rule with various tricks. I would prolong television time as long as possible, but when my father's serious voice told me to go to bed, I would; but not because he told me to, because I decided that I wanted to go to bed. My dad really wanted to spend some alone time with my mom, but I still wanted my mom to tuck me in. So after I went to bed as told, I would call out, "Mom … MOM … *MOOOMM* …" in increasing length and volume.

Then I would hear my dad's voice say, "What is it?"

Under my breath, I would say, "I wasn't calling you! I want MOM!" But instead I would call, "Mom, can you come here?" When I heard her footsteps headed toward my room, I wiggled in my sheets in excitement until she filled up my doorway with her silhouette. I was so glad. I hated being alone.

"Yes, Holly Hocks?" she would ask.

"Can you read to me?"

She knew what I was up to, but she would kneel down beside my bed and lay her hand on my forehead and gently pet me. I never wanted her to leave.

I missed her so much right now that I thought I might cry. I thought I was crying because I could hear it, but then I realized that it wasn't me crying. I tried to listen extra hard to find the source. I thought it was coming from one of the other girls. Maybe she was missing her mom, too. I felt sorry for whoever it was and tried to figure out who it could be. The cries sounded kind of like a baby calling for help. It was muffled. Maybe the person was crying into their pillow. I wanted to get up and find who was crying, but I thought I should stay put. Eventually the sounds slowly stopped and I was finally able to get to sleep for a short while anyway, until ....

* * *

Morning bells went off entirely too early. They clanged around in my head so rudely that I woke up in a bad, dragon-like mood. I wanted to breathe fire on whoever set that despicable alarm. It seemed that I slept for only thirty minutes. In fact, it was still dark out. What time was it? My eyes and head ached as I tried to figure out the time. I was being rushed out of bed and made to get dressed.

We formed a groggy line at the door. I realized I didn't have my glasses on and I quickly grabbed them. We were all brought to a wing of the house that I didn't even know existed yesterday. I noticed the thumbsucker standing by the door; she looked so much older with her thumb out of her mouth. She had a little smile on her face when she looked at me. I made the effort to smile back and she said, "Nice hair," as she rolled her eyes. I felt my hair and it must have been sticking up into the air like bolts of lightning surging away from my scalp. I tried to push it down. I caught a glimpse in the windowpane as we walked past. Where was my bunny hat when I needed it? I shrugged my shoulders and decided to let gravity do the work for me.

My group was brought into a room filled with unmade beds and messes everywhere. The room looked so out of place considering that the rest of the house was so grand and neat. Miss Place informed us of what she expected. We were instructed to clean the room spotlessly and make the beds as demonstrated in the film we had seen. I hadn't paid a lot of attention to the film so I conjured up the formula I used on my own bed from the previous evening.

For the next couple of hours, we all worked together to clean the room and make the beds. We thought we were finished and called for inspection. Miss Place came in, looked around and mumbled, "You call this clean?" She tapped a long stick on the posts of the beds as she paced from one end of the room to the other. "Not even close," she said as she walked out.

With her return, she had a group of other staff members mess up all the beds. They did this systematically, moving from bed to bed like invaders going from house to house looking for victims to torment. I guessed the victims were halfway-nicely-made beds. They practically destroyed the beds and put all the sheets and covers in a pile in the center of the room. That would make things harder for sure. After they were finished with the raid, they told us we had to clean the room all over again. So we did it again. And then they messed it up again … and again … and again.

The cycle continued. I was starved and I could smell the food coming from the dining hall. At this point, I would have eaten a pile of livers and earthworms, I was so hungry. I felt like I was going to pass out. But then we broke for lunch.

I opened my brown bag, ready to devour whatever they had given me, when I realized that my lunch was what I hadn't eaten yesterday. I thought I threw that away. I looked at the trash cans and saw Miss Shapen shaking her clear-gloved finger, warning me to never throw good food away.

Phooey.

My food looked the same, only with a few nibbles off the sides. It was day-old cold ham chunks, even browner apples, and more wilted lettuce cheese wraps … again. Yuck. My stomach groaned in protest. I was starving, but this looked so gross.

"Same food, huh?" Staniel and Danley came to sit with me with trays of new, beautiful food. "Do yourself a favor and just eat it before it gets more rotten," they warned me. "Nothing goes to waste. It's a lesson best learned sooner than later."

"How long have you guys been here?"

"Not long … but long enough."

I caught their drift and painfully swallowed the old food. It went down a lot easier because I was so hungry, but when it was all gone, I felt queasy. The uneasy feeling was magnified when I looked at the next table and I saw a boy, who must have thought he was all alone, pick his nose. At first, he was toying with the idea, but then he was digging around so aggressively, his nostrils were being pulled apart like putty. He used his index finger and then switched to his pinky. It looked like he had grown out his pinky nail specifically for this type of excavation. He was successful. He examined his treasure, talked to it, saying, "Hey there, little guy, you look tasty." And then he ate it. I turned my head just as he realized his snack/buddy time was witnessed. I didn't want to embarrass him or, more importantly, barf.

THE CHILDREN'S HORRIBLE HOUSE

CHAPTER 13
YOU WILL BE TESTED

I was happy that lunch was over, but not so happy because we were ushered into our first class. We filed in like ants in a parade, filling each row from left to right. I was sitting in the precise middle of the classroom. The teacher would have a direct view of me. Written on the board in cursive handwriting, Miss Spelling introduced herself.

Hello! My name is Miss Spelling.

She was a tall woman with a full figure, who appeared very sturdy but not threatening. Her silver-streaked hair crowned her head in plummeting curling tendrils, like Little Bo Peep, and her violet, half-moon–shaped eyes were kind. Her first name was Story, and she was wearing carrot-shaped earrings.

Her voice floated out of her mouth in melodic rhythms. She introduced us to the subjects we would be studying: astronomy, horticulture, and meteorology. She told us how we would be learning each subject individually, but eventually each subject would intersect and complement one another. They sounded like languages

I couldn't comprehend. I felt like I was too young to learn about them. At my school, it was reading, writing, and arithmetic, and I was relatively new to even those. And let's just say I wasn't what anyone would call an intellectual. How would I possibly understand these subjects? I started to get nervous. Miss Spelling would have no choice but to fail me and I would be stuck here forever, until some of her words spoke louder than my fearful thoughts of inadequacy. As she began to explain them, they sounded more like stars and planets, gardening, and weather.

The next words she spoke were: "There will be no tests." This became my new favorite sentence in the world.

What? Could you please repeat that? I questioned silently, but she seemed to pick up on my question telepathically because she said it again.

"There will be no tests. But that does not mean that you won't be tested."

Okay, now I was confused. I thought she said there would be no tests, but we would be tested? How is that possible?

Again, she must be a mind reader, because she asked, "How is this possible? I'll tell you how it is possible. Each lesson each day will have a direct link to your day-to-day activities. If you have paid attention, you will pass easily; but if you don't pay attention, failure will be certain. With each passing task, you will receive a reward. A lot of times you won't be aware of your reward until you do not pass and the things you took for granted will be taken from you. I hope I'm not scaring you. I'm sure you will all do your best." Her mouth closed and her lips spread to a sweet smile.

After a pause, she turned to her desk and picked up a stack of papers. She handed them out and when I got mine, I looked at it and immediately I was extremely confused, because if I was not mistaken, this looked exactly like a test. She explained to us that this was just an evaluation of what we already knew. It was multiple choice. As I looked at the questions, I thought they weren't as hard as I'd feared. I read each question thoroughly to be sure I understood before I answered. This was unusual for me; I normally skimmed the questions and gave my best guess, but I didn't want to fail this—whatever it was called—test or evaluation. When I was finished, I looked up and saw that everyone else was finished as well. We handed the papers forward and she collected them from each row. The time actually flew by in class. She briefly covered and summarized what we would be learning about the subjects and told us that more fun awaited us tomorrow. Strangely, I was excited to come back.

CHAPTER 14

Many Moons Ago at

The North Star Estate

Saffron decided she was ready to leave her home, but she didn't have any money. She knew her father would give her money, and she had to use the right strategy.

She walked around his study and stopped in front of the tall arched window that took up one whole wall. It was almost dark out, yet she could see the tall oak tree that she used to climb, graciously extending its branches, trying to lure her, but she had no time to spare.

"I've decided to design and plant a garden," she said.

Hawthorne's eyes lit up as if she had told him that Sings-in-the-Meadow was coming home, or that she loved him. His eyes fluttered and his mouth quivered before his words could exit. She may have excited him too much, she realized, as she walked back toward his desk.

"Have you? I'll help you, of course!" He started to get up.

"No, no!" she exclaimed as she nudged him back down. "I want to do this myself … I mean, I want to do this for you," she said in the sweetest voice she could muster.

"Oh, okay. Well, I would love to give you any assistance necessary to help you succeed," he said as he flipped through his giant book, looking for some gardening information he had recorded.

"Great. I'll need $1,000.00 to get started," she said with her expectant hand extended and a beaming smile.

He chortled and asked, "What kind of garden are you planning? One for the queen of England?"

"No," she said, "a majestic garden for the king of The North Star Estate."

It pleased her father to think that Saffron would plant a garden for him and it erased all earlier concerns he had. He seemed excited and eager to fulfill this desire. He reached into his right-hand desk drawer and counted out a thousand dollars and almost gave it to her.

"Who is going to help you?" he quickly asked.

She grabbed the money and said, "If I need help, I will ask Reed." He was their butler and she knew her father trusted him. Hawthorne agreed with a nod.

* * *

Saffron carelessly drew up plans for the honorary garden. Without realizing it, she found that she actually enjoyed planning it out. It was as if gardening was part of her being. She made a maze of viburnum that encircled the inner garden that would hold, of what she could remember, her mother's favorite plants. Saffron knew she loved fruit-bearing trees like apples, nectarines, plums, and kumquats. She included some of the medicinal plants that her mother taught her about, like camphor, lavender, and lemongrass. She also included some flowering shrubs and giant chestnut trees. Some ornamental plants, like hollyhocks and daisies, were planned to follow the pathways that led to the giant weeping willow that would greet all who entered. After drawing the tree, she stopped and stared at it. Saffron embodied the steadfast sadness the tree symbolized. Her vision blurred as teardrops grew heavier, until hitting the paper below the weeping willow, blotting the drawing to appear as if there were a reflecting pond beneath the tree. How regrettably ironic, she thought.

After her fleeting emotion faded, she held out the drawing for inspection. She taped it onto her wall and stood back. She imagined it in all its potential beauty. Saffron realized she would never bring this fantasy garden to fruition as she ripped it down from the wall, crumpled it up, and threw it on the ground. She focused her eyes on the balled-up paper and made her real plans.

After the house became quiet, she deliberately made her room look like it had been ransacked. She flung her clothes around and messed up her bed to make it look like there was a struggle. She cocked the pictures and smeared soot on the wall. She wrote in red, dripping, nail polish: "Your daughter is gone."

Saffron crept back into the study and opened the top right-hand drawer. There was a stack of bills, all big ones. She grabbed them all and snuck out of the study undetected. As she was tiptoeing out,

Saffron tripped over the doll that looked like her mother. She picked it up and looked at it for a moment before tossing it aside as if it had no meaning. She opened her window, letting in a crisp, smoke-filled gulp of air. The breeze felt rebellious and refreshing. Her hair floated around her head, suspended by micro gusts as she climbed down the jessamine lattice, onto the first-floor porch roof. She leaped off the roof, onto an oak tree politely offering its branch. She climbed down the trunk and ran across the pebbled driveway before squeezing through the iron gate. The trees bent around her fleeing form while the illuminated torches lit the path as she ran away.

CHAPTER 15
THE DUNGEON

After class, we were brought back to the chamber room we had spent all morning cleaning, to find it was now a huge mess again. We cleaned it again and again; it was still not good enough. I wondered if it would be like this forever. I heard someone humming a tune. It sounded familiar. I listened hard as more kids began to join in. It was slow, deep, and it gave me chills. One girl's spooky voice shone through, causing goose pimples to pop out from my skin. It was then that I recognized the tune and joined in with the rest of the cleaning crew.

"The Children's Horrible House
The Children's Horrible House
Where you work all day and never, never play …
The Children's Horrible House …"

Someone added a new verse:

> *"You better do your job,*
> *you ungrateful slob …*
> *The Children's Horrible House …"*

Singing the song while making the beds turned out to make time pass fluidly. We were all in this mess together and somehow it brought everyone closer. But this feeling would soon fade.

> *"You better make beds right*
> *or you'll be up all night …*
> *The Children's Horrible House …"*

While we were cleaning the chamber again, a girl named Yarrow, who looked like a deflated tubular balloon, started to complain.

"How many times are we going to have to do this?" she asked. "I'm sick of this song. This is stupid," she whined.

I supposed she didn't much care for our singalong.

Miss Place, who was standing guard as we worked, grabbed her by the arm and told her, "Well, Yarrow, since you're sick of cleaning the room, making beds, and singing, maybe you should go to **THE DUNGEON** and see how you like it there."

The hairs on my arms stood up.

Miss Place and Yarrow went out the door and down the hall.

THE DUNGEON? What's that? I wondered. I didn't know there was a dungeon. And what is a dungeon, anyway? It sounds creepy. Was this how we knew we didn't pass the test? There was only one way to find out.

I followed them. I walked on the very tip of my toes to make as little noise as possible. I stepped quietly down the stairs. When I made it to the bottom floor, I noticed how this part of the house looked carved out of the earth itself. The walls were brown and solid, like petrified bricks of dirt. I peeked around the corner before I made my way in pursuit.

There were no windows, so gas-filled torches lit the hallways. At the last corner, there was a long hallway and at the end was a black iron door that Miss Place knocked on seven times. I knew this knock. My brothers and sisters used to sing, "Shave and a haircut, two bits," all the time. It was the same rhythm. The door reluctantly squealed open and in they went. It shut with a thunderous clunk.

Above the door frame hung another carved wooden plaque that read:

Never Let Your Fear
Decide Your Fate

After I was sure the door was closed, I scurried up and put my ear against it. At first I couldn't hear a thing. But then, I heard it.

"Whack!"... Then, crying.

I heard footsteps getting closer, so I ran. I ran around the corner just in time for the door to creak open. I ran back up the flights of stairs and through the maze of hallways, back to the cleaning room, and cleaned and made the bed better than I thought I ever could.

As Miss Place returned with Yarrow and her tear-streaked face, Miss Place took notice of my bed. Her eyebrow raised and she came to my bed and said, "Nice job."

She turned to everyone in the room and told them all to stop. She said, "At least one of you here is understanding the process. I want each of you to look at Holly's bed. This is what I expect from each of you. Now that Holly, who has only been here a short time, has demonstrated that a nicely made bed is possible, maybe going to **THE DUNGEON** will remind you that putting some effort into your chore will be better than doing your chore with a blistered behind!"

She lined everyone up to go. "Not you, Holly. You don't need to go. The rest of you do."

I didn't mean for them all to get in trouble. But when they reappeared, I think they thought I did. I could see the anger and hatred in their eyes. They blamed me.

I wasn't sure I liked passing these tests.

CHAPTER 16
LIGHTS OUT

No one talked to me for the rest of the day. When I went to bed that night, I felt even more alone than I did the first night. I felt really sorry for myself, and this time I did cry. No one liked me and I could hear them all talking about me as if I was the dumbest, ugliest, most disgusting person on the planet. Even the thumb-sucker seemed disgusted by me.

I turned toward the window and wondered what Dookie was doing. Was he missing me? Who was feeding my hamster and changing his cedar chips? I knew Ginger wouldn't care about Dookie. But my mom probably would. My mom had to be the nicest mom in the world. I started thinking about when I was smaller. She would pick me up and swing me in her arms, acting like she was going to toss me. I would squeal like a warthog when she would tickle me by burying her face in the nape of my neck. As I succumbed to a huge amount of nostalgia, a star streamed across the sky right before my eyes. I suddenly felt hope and knew my mom was near in spirit. I imagined her as a tiny fairy flying across the sky, like that shooting star. I thought back to when we were at camp, deep in the woods, away from all lights. We all lay back with our faces pointed to the starlit sky. There were so many stars out that it didn't seem real. My mom would point out the different constellations. I couldn't remember them all, but I was sure she knew all of them. This shooting star was a message from my mom telling me to be brave and that I could get through this.

Just when I was feeling better, I heard the cries again. I knew it wasn't me because I was feeling pretty good. I felt bad for whoever it was. I thought maybe I should go look for the source and see if I could help.

I got out of bed and followed the sound. It seemed to be coming from the walls, and then I realized they were coming from the vents placed throughout the house. The venting system acted like a system of veins that carried sound from one source, throughout the whole place like a heart would for a body. I went down the halls and as I went, I listened for the source. Before I knew it, I was standing in front of THE DUNGEON.

Humph. I never thought that a dungeon would be so vital. Perhaps it was the stomach of the house, always grumbling and groaning, whether full or empty. But you don't get spanked in your belly, so maybe it was the butt … that made noises too. It made sense … that *is* where you get spanked, on your butt. And getting spanked always made me cry. But who was getting spanked in the middle of the night in THE DUNGEON? I thought it was "lights out" for everyone.

I touched the handle of the door, but I was too scared to turn it. It was cold and stiff, like me, as a chill ran down my spine and my body stiffened in fear. I thought about opening the door, but I was afraid of being attacked by whoever was inside. Do crying people attack? I remembered my mom telling me that hurt dogs will often bite someone who is trying to help them. Then from behind the door, I heard silence. The crying stopped and I didn't hear more.

Sometimes, silence is even more frightening, I learned. As I climbed back upstairs I kept hearing phantom noises. I would look back expecting to see a ghostly goblin chasing me. I was walking as fast as possible, until the hairs on my arms stood up like there was static in the air. My feet and legs scrambled clumsily; it seemed as if I couldn't get coordinated fast enough.

After I got to my room, I dive-bombed my bed and hid under the covers, shaking myself to sleep.

CHAPTER 17
THE GHOST

Even though I fell asleep under questionable circumstances, I slept like a caterpillar in a chrysalis. When I woke up, I felt like a new being. I was hesitant to leave my pillowed, private cocoon.

At morning work, I cleaned and made the beds as quickly as possible. I couldn't wait for lunch. My stomach was grumbling like a homeless hobo. You cannot imagine my relief when the dining bell rang. I sat down with a nice, fresh lunch and ate it like it was the best cafeteria food that had ever been prepared. I looked over at Miss Shapen and thanked her with a wide smile. She blinked heavily in response.

After Staniel and Danley came to sit with me, they told me to "Breathe … take a sip of water! You're inhaling your food!"

"Hey, did you guys know about THE DUNGEON?" I asked with a mouthful of food.

Both of their faces turned down in disgust at the sight of my half-chewed food, but then they answered, "Yeah."

"Have you ever gone to THE DUNGEON?" This time, I had waited until my food was completely chewed and swallowed.

"No."

"Do you know anyone who has?"

"Yeah." Their answers were always this brief.

"Who?"

"Steve Leeves, but he left," Danley informed me.

"Steve Leeves? Well, I guess that makes sense."

My food was staring back at me, waiting to be devoured, so I continued eating ... but then I began to wonder .... "Have you guys heard the crying at night?"

"Used to, but now we tune it out," Staniel said.

"Do you know who it is?" I asked while trying to decide if I should go ahead and eat my banana pudding now or wait until I finished my noodles.

"We heard it was a ghost."

"A ghost?" I gasped. I knew it! Actually, if I knew it was a ghost I may not have been so brave. "Who told you it was a ghost?"

"Everyone here knows about the ghost. It's not a big deal. It cries every night and once in a while something creepy happens, but overall it's not a problem," Danley assured me.

I was not as casual as they were about the idea of ghosts. I mean, this place looked perfect for haunting, and the idea of a ghost isn't that scary, but when you could actually encounter one, that was a different story. I recalled my phantom ghostly encounter last night and I must have lost all the color in my face because the boys tried to make me feel better.

"It's okay, Holly," Danley said. "We think the ghost is harmless. It doesn't appear to want to scare us or the other kids. It seems more interested in something else. It's like it lives here, for some reason."

I needed more information. "Tell me, why is this ghost crying?"

Again, Danley answered. "See that picture up on the wall over there?" They both pointed to the portrait of Hawthorne North Star.

"Yes." I decided this was a good time to dig into my pudding. "Go on," I prodded.

But the bell rang, indicating that lunch was over.

"See, he had a daughter, named Saffron; she's the ghost, we think. This used to be her home, but the story goes, she was kidnapped. Some people say she ran away, but when she returned, her father was gone."

They took turns informing me until Miss Shapen and her jiggly body practically threw us out of the dining hall.

CHAPTER 18
The Paddles

Ughhhh. I wanted to know more, but I had to wait. I gobbled down the rest of my pudding and put away my tray.

In my new class, I noticed Clover sitting in front of Cherry. Cherry was chirping in her ear like a magpie. I wondered what they were talking about. I noticed Clover blinking and shrugging her shoulders as she had before, but seeing her from afar, I wondered if her movements were involuntary, like a tic of some sort. It didn't change my feelings; it actually made me laugh a little and appreciate her more. She was unique in a funny way. I started to copy her movements and when she looked over at me, I exaggerated them more to mess around with her, but when she realized what I was doing, she clamped her lips together and looked away.

Class that day became very interesting. Miss Gyde, our astronomy teacher, was very different from Miss Spelling, who was tall and friendly. Miss Gyde was younger and on the short side. Her white-blonde hair and dainty tipped toes made her look like a comet. She was built like one carefully melded muscle. When it came to teaching, she was straight to the point; no fluff, just the facts. As it turned out, I appreciated her style as well. She introduced us to astronomy in more detail. I really liked it. It's the study of outer space. She drew some constellations on the blackboard and I could see her muscles flexing around even in her small movements.

I liked the Big Dipper. It looked like a big shopping basket, open for holding clusters of other stars and constellations. I was really going to like this class. She showed us a movie about how the three pyramids in Giza, Egypt, are mirrored in the sky by the three stars on Orion's Belt. I had never imagined that people in ancient times would be observant enough to build things in direct correlation to the stars. It was so amazing to think that mankind could construct something so brilliant. I wondered if people were smarter in ancient times.

* * *

Afternoon work went similarly to morning work. I couldn't wait for dinner, or D-Hall, as we began to call it. As I was doing my chores, I could hear someone being taken to THE DUNGEON. At least, that's what I figured, because Mr. Meanor was leading a boy down the hall in that direction, and the boy's face was a mix of defiance and fear. I decided I should follow them to see what was going on. This time, I wasn't as stealthy as the last time.

Mr. Meanor turned around and said, in his mean old grumbly tone, "Do you want to go to **THE DUNGEON** as well?"

I shook my head *no* as I looked down. When I looked up they were gone. Phew, that was close. I wonder how hard they spank. My dad could spank pretty hard. In fact, if you didn't cry the first time, like my sister Ginger decided to do once, he spanked harder.

The time when Ginger got spanked was when all the kids were being bad at dinner. So he lined us all up—except for me, because I was sick. I had the flu and my mom set me up on a blanket near the dinner table. My brothers started it, Hickory mostly. Hickory instigated by putting something gross on Cashew's plate and snickering about his deed. Cashew reacted by telling on him and then refusing to eat his dinner. Juniper mimicked Cashew by repeating him in an exaggerated whine, "Mom! Hickory just wiped a booger on my plate! And now it's all gross and now I can't eat. ... *Wah, wah.*" And Ginger laughed; not a cute little laugh, but a big guffaw. This combination would first get "the hairy eyeball," as we called it, from my dad.

My dad had a way of looking at us that in general would make us sit up straight and be quiet. My dad had horrible eyesight. He has worn thick glasses since he was six months old. When he read something, he took *off* his glasses and held the paper close to his eyes. When we were bad, he took off his glasses and gave us a stern stare that often made one of his eyes wander. But on the occasion that the *hairy eyeball* didn't work, he counted on his raised voice to get our attention. For instance, he would say, "HEY! Knock it off!" But when that failed, there was only one thing left ... the PADDLE! We hated the paddle! But every now and then he gave us a reminder.

This time, he said, "Okay, that's enough! I want you all to clear your plates and line up."

First it was Hickory. Whack!

"Boo-hoo."

Hickory knew that if you didn't cry, more would come.

Then it was Cashew. Whack!

"Boo-hoo."

Cashew knew it also.

Juniper was third. Whack!

"Boo-hoo."

Juniper caught on early.

Lastly, it was Ginger's turn. Whack!

"YOWL," she said with what sounded like a giggle.

Whack!

"YOWL," she said again.

We were all in shock. What was she doing?

Whack!

"YOWL," she howled, but this time there was no giggle.

"Ginger, you have to cry, or it gets harder," Cashew whispered.

Whack!

"Boo-hoo."

Finally, she got the point and never *yowled* again.

There were some perks to being the youngest. I did a lot of observations of what not to do, but that didn't always keep me out of trouble. I hoped to be observant enough here at The Children's Horrible House, too.

CHAPTER 19

The North Star Estate

Hawthorne North Star was devastated. His butler, Reed Trustworthy, told him about the kidnapping. They called the police and put out an all-points bulletin on Saffron Radiant Star. They described her clothes, height, and hair and eye color. She had last been seen in long, dark slacks and a flowered tunic. She was five-foot-seven-inches tall and had long, dark hair with honey-dipped ends. Her bright hazel eyes often appeared to be the same color as her name, Saffron. She bore an uncanny resemblance to her mother's striking features, such as her high cheekbones and rosy lips, but *her* almond-shaped eyes had a bit of a twinkle that made them appear mischievous.

The most recent painting of her was when she was a child. It was a painted portrait with her mother, Sings-in-the-Meadow. Hawthorne was touching the faces in the portrait as if he were blind and it was painted in braille. His wife, Sings-in-the-Meadow, had gone back to live with her people some time ago and he still grieved. The extravagant life he provided for her was not enough; in truth, it was too much.

When she left, it was like their daughter's spirit began to wander away in search of her missing mother. He wanted a piece of his beloved wife and was grateful for his daughter's staying, but he felt so much guilt about not being able to keep them together as a family. He tried to overcompensate for the loss, but it seemed to make things worse. He loved his daughter very much and wanted to give her anything she wished for. He commissioned the biggest dollhouse imaginable, furnished with elaborate trimmings. He even had the whole attic turned into a giant playroom. He filled it with toys and gifts and everything a child could ever want, but she had outgrown these things.

Hawthorne went up in the attic to see if he could find any clue as to where Saffron had gone. He carefully placed each one of the toys she had discarded in its proper position. When he came to the dollhouse, he saw a male doll alone in the study, resting at the desk. Where were all the other dolls? Up in the attic of the dollhouse was the mother doll holding the baby doll. He realized Saffron had placed them like this, causing his grief to compound. Hawthorne wept.

* * *

She seemed to be okay, he had told himself, but she wasn't. Nothing could replace her mother; he knew that. He thought that the garden she was planning would bring a new beginning for them. They would finally have a common ground that even linked them to her mother. Sings-in-the-Meadow and Hawthorne together were passionate about growing crops and plants in abundance. He hoped in all earnestness that Sings-in-the-Meadow would return, but deep down he knew she never would.

THE CHILDREN'S HORRIBLE HOUSE

CHAPTER 20
THE CHILDREN'S HORRIBLE HOUSE
A PUPPY PLAYDATE

That night at dinner, we had a fourth person at our table. I saw
Clover walking with her tray, looking for someone, and I guessed it
was Cherry. But she couldn't seem to find her.

I stood and looked for Cherry too, but no luck. "Hey, Clover,
want to sit with us?"

She walked slowly to our table, still in search. "Gawsh, I wonda'
where Cherry is?" she said.

The twins shrugged. I didn't know where she was either, but I
was a little glad. Nothing against Cherry, but deep down I wished for
a best friend like Clover.

I introduced Clover to the twins and they all seemed to like each
other. But Clover had something in her mouth that needed to come out.

"Hey," she said, addressing the twins, "how did you get your
names, Staniel and Danley?"

The twins looked at each other, shrugged, and said, "Our mom's name is Danielle and our dad's name is Stanley. They put them together and voilà!"

It sounded as if they had said it a million times before.

"So, what's your last name?" I asked.

"PricklyPear," they both stated.

"You are a prickly pair, that's for sure," I teased.

Clover agreed, and their dimples appeared along with their smiles.

We were eating our food when *someone* brought up dogs again, and the way she said "dawg" made me spit my food out as I laughed. I wiped my face and uniform as she asked if I had a dog.

"Kinda," I said. "Well, my sister's boyfriend gave her a dog—a Pomeranian."

"No way! I have a Pomeranian!" she exclaimed.

This made her light up. But the truth was I didn't really care for Filbert (that was our dog's name, but it was pronounced "Fil-bair" with a silent *t*, as if he were "Frawnch," to sound more fancy). He was extraordinarily cute, but he peed everywhere and he pooped on my bed once. And my sister blamed me! She said that *I* had pooped on my bed, but I hadn't. Who would poop on their own bed? He never came when you called him and he would come when you didn't want him, like if you were changing your clothes, he would take your underwear and rip it to shreds.

Clover seemed really excited about Filbert, so I didn't say anything. She told me she had a black female Pomeranian, named Pepper.

"She's such a good dawg. She sleeps with me every night and she neva' makes messes. Maybe we can get our dawgs to meet one day. They can have a puppy playdate." Clover smiled as she clapped her hands.

We pretty much talked for the rest of lunchtime. I liked making her laugh. She told me that she was blind in one eye. I guess that's why she blinked so much and why her eyes didn't always line up. Clover's bad eye often lingered on an object or person a little longer than her good eye. She blinked in order to make it follow her good eye.

"So, if you close your left eye, what can you see?" I asked.

"Nothin', just like if you closed both of your eyes."

I told her to close her left eye, but to keep the right one open.

At first she tilted her head, judging whether or not to trust me.

"I promise I won't hurt you," I assured her.

She closed her eye, and I told her to put her hand over it. With her right eye opened but not focused on anything, I waved my hand back and forth. The eyeball didn't move. I then pointed my finger really close to her eye and she only blinked when my finger touched her eyelash.

"What ahh you doin'?" she asked as she pulled back.

"Oh, you really are blind." My disbelief was gone.

"Duh."

"Wow." I was confounded. "So you only see half of what I see?"

"Actually, it has always confused me to think about how you see out of two eyes. I would think that it would be like two different pictures or that it would be all blurry or somethin'. My eye has always been blind and I see one clear picture out of this one," she said, pointing.

I put a hand over one of my eyes, looked around, and decided it wasn't so bad.

"It used to go all over the place." She twirled her finger around, mimicking her previous eye situation.

I laughed as I imagined her eye heedlessly rolling around in her socket.

"I had an operation when I was five years old, to make the blind eye follow the other one."

"Oh, wow! I bet that's a relief, huh?" I was amazed to think about what she had been through.

Dinner was over, and we walked back to my room. She stayed in the room across the hall. Usually we had a little free time after dinner and before bed. We were lying on my bed talking about our homes and our families when the two jerks decided to show up. Even though I knew their real names, I personally referred to them as Bucktooth and Hillbilly.

"Ew, what are you doing?" Bucktooth asked.

"Ew, they're in bed together," Hillbilly added.

I wasn't sure how to reply, and Clover said nothing. Because of her unusually deep voice, I thought she was tough when I first met her, but after getting to know her, I decided she was a big softy. I understood what they were implying, but it wasn't true. From a very young age, I sometimes worried about how ugly I was and my brother Cashew would assure me, saying, "One day, Holly Hocks, you will blossom into a beautiful flower." I clung to this promise.

Clover and I tried to ignore them, but they wouldn't go away.

"Ew, they're gonna kissth!" bucktoothed Thistle shouted.

We both jolted up, and I said, "We are not! We are just friends."

"Oh yeah? Well, you look like more than friendsth." They thought this was hysterical.

We decided it would be best if we went to Clover's room. When we walked in, Cherry was waiting for Clover and as soon as Clover saw her, I seemed to disappear. Both their faces lit up as they greeted one another and they started yapping again, like the first time I saw them. I stood there waiting for them to notice me, but when I made a suggestive shuffle with my feet, they briefly looked at me, and then their backs closed on me like elevator doors.

That wasn't my favorite feeling. The day that had started out so great was fizzling to one of the worst. Why were friends the best and the worst source of anguish? So I didn't seem so desperate, I let myself out of their room and went back to my own. I found comfort in my nest and settled in for the night.

CHAPTER 21
The North Star Estate

Hawthorne's spirit and health had declined in the aftermath of his daughter's disappearance. He was sure that she would will her way back home if she were alive. Saffron was a strong-willed child. He stayed in bed for weeks. His depression was apparent to his butler. Like a most treasured friend, Reed was there for Hawthorne if he ever decided to talk.

One day after much time had passed, Hawthorne called Reed in and asked him to record his final wishes.

"You're not going to die," Reed argued, in hopes of jolting some life into him.

"No, not yet. But soon I will be gone and I want to put things in order when that day comes."

Reed did as he was asked and wrote down the last will and testament.

* * *

The funeral for Hawthorne North Star was held quietly in private. Before he passed, he had the garden that his daughter had planned for him constructed, and in the center he put a mausoleum where his body would remain. He hoped this would keep them together, even just symbolically. The plans she had drawn up for the garden, he found crumpled near her bed. He carefully spread them out and was awestruck by the detail and natural talent his daughter had for design and drawing. He saw the reflecting pond under the weeping willow and decided he couldn't grow anything other than this fantasy garden constructed in his wife's and his daughter's honor.

CHAPTER 22
THE CHILDREN'S HORRIBLE HOUSE
WHAT ELSE DO WE HAVE TO DO?

Lunchtime couldn't come soon enough. The repetitiousness of making beds and cleaning rooms became a robotic activity. In the dining hall, I rushed to get my food so I could see the twins and Clover.

"Did you guys hear the crying last night?" I asked.

"Is that what that was?" Clover wondered aloud. "I could hear something, but I wasn't sure."

"You guys want to figure out who's crying?" I asked.

"It's the ghost—we already told you," Staniel stated.

"Yes, but are you sure that it is a ghost or ... or that it's the ghost of Saffron Star?"

"N-no, bu-but ...," he said.

"Let's figure out this mystery. I mean, what else do we have to do besides make beds and clean rooms?" Raising my eyebrows, I gave them an urging look.

"Agreed. But how?" Danley asked.

"I was thinking we could follow the sound of the crying first. Then we could figure out who it is," I said.

"What if we get caught?" Clover smartly reminded us.

"Get caught doing what?" Cherry said, and shoved her way between me and Clover.

I didn't really feel like explaining everything to Cherry, so I continued where we'd left off. "Uh, I don't know. We'll think of something. I'm going to figure this out one way or another. You guys in or what?"

Cherry seemed bored by our conversation, judging by the way she mouthed out the word "lame" while picking at her nails and looking around with an overall disinterested expression.

"Guess so," the twins answered.

"Yeah, why not," Clover agreed.

"Count me out." Cherry rolled her eyes, got up, and sauntered away.

"I wasn't asking you," I quietly said like a whispering, puppet-less ventriloquist.

We made a plan that the next time we heard the crying, we would meet in the hallway.

The rest of the day I was filled with anxiety and giddiness. My stomach kept clenching and wrestling around as if it wanted to get out to tell me to *CALM DOWN!* I couldn't wait for evening. At dinner, we planned and mapped out our course and discussed more about how we were going to find this crying ghost.

"It usually starts around ten thirty, I've noticed," Danley informed us.

"Yeah, but it doesn't last long, so we have to be quick if we want to catch it in action," Staniel said, and nodded in agreement with himself.

"Okay. So as soon as we hear the first sign of a cry, let's meet in the hallway outside my room since it's a bit closer to THE DUNGEON," I said.

We put our hands in a circle like we were getting ready for a big game and quietly hurrahed so as not to draw too much attention. But we still giggled at our unnecessary gesture.

* * *

We met our third teacher, Miss Leeds. She was very excited to teach us about meteorology.

"Okay! Class! Find your seats quickly so we can begin!" She said everything as if we were about to leave the room. Her ultraviolet hair was swooped around her head like a cyclone. Her pale blue eyes scanned each one of us like laser beams.

She wasted no time. As soon as everyone was seated, she filled us in on everything we would ever hope to know about the subject.

She began: "Meteorology is the study of the atmosphere, atmospheric phenomena, and atmospheric effects on our weather. The atmosphere is the gaseous layer of the physical environment that surrounds a planet."

She asked us to speak aloud with her as she pointed to her chalkboard, which read: "Earth's atmosphere is roughly 100 to 125 kilometers, or 65–75 miles, thick."

Only a handful of kids obliged.

"Does anyone know how the atmosphere stays put?" she asked. Without waiting for anyone to answer, she took it upon herself, and said, "Gravity!" She jumped. "Gravity keeps the atmosphere from expanding farther, just like it won't let me fly away as I jump."

She stopped jumping, took a breath, and flipped her chart to a picture of Earth and its atmosphere. It was like a visible invisible concept, as if a thought became visible in a bubble that surrounded my head. I hadn't thought about gravity or our atmosphere before, and now I couldn't stop thinking about it. She asked if anyone knew where most weather took place.

No one raised their hand, so she answered herself.

"That's right! In these lower parts of our atmosphere and, coincidentally, that is where meteorology focuses on." She pointed to the area on her chart.

"So why is the study of meteorology so important?" she prompted.

All I heard were crickets.

"Yup," she affirmed, "to observe, explain, and forecast our weather. And what depends on our weather?"

"Everything," a voice from somewhere spoke.

Everyone looked around for the speaker and then all eyes landed on me. *Did I say that?* I must have, because Miss Leeds gave me an appreciative smile, and agreed.

"She's right. Everything depends on our weather. Meteorologists use scientific principles to observe, explain, and forecast our weather. They also research the relationship between the atmosphere and Earth's climates, oceans, and biological life. Forecasters use that data to make predictions."

She continued with more charts and diagrams. All this information was starting to clog my brain. I needed to flush some of it down my throat, as well as use the bathroom, and lucky for me, Miss Leeds' class was soon over.

CHAPTER 23
SHHHH!

We seemed really brave at dinner, but when it came time for action, that was a different story. That night, I waited in my bed, listening for the sounds. I was pretty sure my house was haunted. It was well over one hundred years old and it had tales to tell in each creaking board and squealing door opening. Come to think of it, The Children's Horrible House had a lot of those, too. I guess when you hear the same noises all the time, they seem less noticeable.

I focused my senses and became more aware of the noises around me. It was like the whole building was breathing in and out. With each labored breath, the house invited me to go explore. Then I heard it: the invitation I was waiting for, but I was scared to accept. The cries for help began, louder than I had heard before.

I bounced out of bed and put on my robe and socks. This was part of our strategy to go undetected. I impatiently tapped my foot on the floor as I waited for the gang. Clover was rubbing her eyes as she showed up. I was relieved when Cherry wasn't with her.

Clover yawned and said, "Where are the PP twins?"

Cherry called them this because their last name was PricklyPear, and it had caught on. Staniel and Danley slid in like they were doing a burnout. Clover and I smiled, and I signaled for them to follow me. We practically skated on the polished wooden floors. We descended the stairs. When we got to the hallway which led to **THE DUNGEON**, we stopped and surveyed the hall before continuing. The twins were touching the walls, wondering what they were made of.

Clover suddenly sounded unsure. "I think we should go back to bed," she said.

I was scared too, but then I noticed the carved wooden plaque again.

Never Let Your Fear
Decide Your Fate

I wondered why it was all the way down here. It was a sign telling us to be brave, while it was surrounded by creepiness. In the dining room of my house, my parents had a carved wooden plaque that read:

> *Some hae meat and canna eat*
> *Some wad eat who want it*
> *But we hae meat and we can eat*
> *So let the Lord be thankit.*

This saying often puzzled me and I read it over and over so many times that I had it memorized.

"Shhhh!" I warned, even though no one had made a sound. It must have been the voice inside my head that was being so loud. They all looked at me with confused expressions. I tried to apologize facially.

The cries were less intense, but we could still hear them. I put my ear up against the door as something crashed to the floor from behind the door. Then I heard, "Oh, dear …."

It was a lady's voice.

We all jumped and clambered back up the stairs, back to our rooms, and into our beds—so much for our earlier bravery. I was breathing hard; my heart was racing. I was disappointed in myself because I didn't find out any new information.

I had a hard time settling down. I kept replaying the sound of the ghost's voice in my head and then picturing us all running away like raccoons. I promised myself and that sign I would be braver next time.

I needed to get to sleep, so I closed my eyes and pictured sheep jumping through the starlit sky. My mixed-up mind was picturing sheep in **THE DUNGEON**, counting bones—not a pleasant thought. I shook my head and concentrated my gaze out into the nighttime sky. For a brief moment, I thought about sucking my thumb, but then realized how ridiculous I would look and feel. So I thought about comforting things, like my security blanket that I had had when I was much smaller. It was just a rag, but to me it had a certain calming scent and its name was Istis. See, when I was little, Juniper and Cashew pretended that my blanket was lost and when we found it, they said, "Here it is!" But since I was small and couldn't speak clearly, I repeated, "Istis!" My conjuring seemed to work. I was able to fall asleep while recalling the comforting scent of Istis.

CHAPTER 24
The North Star Estate

The North Star Estate went through an entire alteration process upon the passing of Hawthorne North Star. Even though the structure was the same, it was no longer a home for the Star family. It would be home for children who, like Saffron, had gone astray. Before he passed, Hawthorne realized that even though he loved his daughter very much, the lack of discipline—as evidenced by her messy room and unmade bed—had caused her to spin out of control. In his heart of hearts, he knew it was his fault. He wanted to make amends for not doing the right thing for his daughter. So he decided since it was too late to help her, he would help as many children as he could. He would also be helping parents like him from feeling the guilt and pain for which he found no absolution.

He gave his North Star Estate over to the state and made sure his most esteemed butler, Reed Trustworthy, would continue on to care for it, along with his remaining staff. The North Star Estate was now called *The Hawthorne House for Children*. It was a full-time reform school which retaught obedience skills through the most basic tasks and chores: making beds, cleaning rooms, and doing dishes, as well as educating children on the ancient gifts of knowledge that he and his Sings-in-the-Meadow had studied.

Hawthorne had thought back to his early years, when his life was much simpler. He came from a modest family, and when he set out on his own, his former uncomplicated existence, in hindsight, was preferable. He realized that life was better when it was not so complicated by wealth. All the money and the things became a stranglehold on him and it ruined his family. He couldn't hug or embrace his things. And the loved ones he wished to embrace were driven away by those things. He wished he could go back in time and make up for the problems he and his accumulation of wealth had caused. He found that this was the only way he could make amends for his foolishness.

In some ways, he accomplished his goal through his last wish.

CHAPTER 25
THE CHILDREN'S HORRIBLE HOUSE FREE DAY

One morning, I woke up and the sun was already out. Did I sleep in? I didn't think we were allowed to do that here. I looked at the clock on the wall. It was just before 8:00 a.m. Usually, we were up and at 'em by six thirty in the morning.

I got out of bed slowly, and asked one of the other girls, Camellia, what was going on.

"Nothing," she answered, not looking up from making her bed.

She had a unique way of tucking in the sheets at the bottom, which made it look neat. I thought maybe I should try to copy that.

"Why is it so late and we aren't going to breakfast or going to clean the rooms?"

"Because it's Sunday."

"Oh!" Wow, I was so used to the routine. "Now what?" I asked as I realized that this was the same girl who told me earlier that she knew me. "You said you knew me earlier, remember?"

"Yeah, but I was mistaken. You just look like someone else."

Someone else looked like me? Poor someone else; I felt bad for that someone.

"Sundays are free days," Camellia said. "You can go outside and play, go to the library and read. The only thing you can't do is nothing."

"What do you mean by nothing?" I asked.

Camellia exhaled, stopped making her bed, and said, "You have to be productive in some way, even if it's fun. You can go outside and play, read a book in the library, or do a group project. The only thing you can't do is lie around and do nothing. If they find you doing nothing, they find something for you to do, and it won't be fun, so I would get going if I were you—after you make your bed, of course."

I took her advice. And I tried to tuck in the sheets the same way she did. I thought I did a good job, until I looked at her perfect bed. It looked so elegant yet effortless. My bed didn't look even close to as good as hers. But it would have to do.

"What are you going to do?" I asked.

She shrugged her shoulders. "Probably go outside, see what's going on out there."

I got dressed and thought about what I was going to do as I went to D-Hall. Alone, I ate quickly and then set out to do some investigating.

CHAPTER 26
THE LIBRARY

For some reason, I was excited about today. I could do whatever I wanted. The possibilities were endless! I walked by the open-air hallway and heard kids playing outside. Some were playing dodgeball and hide-and-seek, while others were playing tag. A group jumping rope was doing the double-dutch while another group had set up hopscotch. It all looked fun and I don't know why I didn't go out to play. Usually, at my school's recess I would be out on the jungle gym doing my single-leg flips for hours. I also loved racing across the monkey bars, but something inside me was drawn to the library that Camellia had mentioned, which is truly out of the ordinary for me. See, I'm more of a tree-climbing, bike-riding, hole-digging kind of girl.

I don't love reading books unless I am forced to read them, but I figured the library would be filled with helpful information. I walked aimlessly until I came up to a staff member. It was Major Whoopins. I hadn't seen him since I got here. I was actually glad to see him and by the glint in his eye, he seemed happy too.

"Wher're you headed, young lady?" he asked.

I was proud to say, "I'm looking for the library." I thought he'd be impressed.

"Okay. It's gon' be on tha' third floor of tha' east wing."

I thanked him and was on my way. As I walked, my body seemed to know where to go. Everything seemed familiar, like I had been here before. Maybe I was having a déjà vu. I saw the grand double doors and noticed the thick panes of glass that went halfway down the otherwise wooden doors. The glass had a circular symbol in the center of the grill. Surrounding the circle were thin strands of metal in a diamond-shaped mesh. On the front of the door, gold letters read: **H. N. STAR LIBRARY**. I grabbed the door handles, pulled them open, and walked in to the biggest, most beautiful library ever.

I guess I was the only one who thought going to the library on our free day was a good idea. I walked around the impressive room. The floors were carpeted in layers of garnet, deep purple, and forest green oriental area rugs going in every direction. A series of tall, arched, heavily cased windows took up one whole wall. The light flooded through the windows in huge sunbeams that lit the enormous room perfectly. The ceiling seemed to be infinite. It was painted blue with clouds which appeared to be moving. There were birds painted mid-flight and, at one point, I thought I could hear them chirping.

The three other walls were floor-to-ceiling books, with ladders on a track making any book accessible. Shelves of books took up the center of the room, and to one side a few tables and chairs were arranged to accommodate study. I didn't know what I was looking for, so at first I just absorbed the elegant, enlightening room. I settled in a large wingback chair behind a monstrous carved wooden desk.

I felt very important all of a sudden. My hand was drawn toward a drawer, but when I went to open it, it was locked.

I imagined being in charge of an important company. I pretended to push a button in order to reach my make-believe secretary, when I heard the door open. Uh-oh, the only thing I was not allowed to do was nothing, and by the looks of me right now, I was doing nothing. I quickly got up, walked toward the bookshelf, and reached for the first book I could find.

Wow, it was heavy—a lot heavier than I expected. It almost fell through my grasp, but I managed to not let it fall. I walked back to my chair and placed it on the desk. Bound in thick leather, the golden embossed title read: *SAGE THEMES*. I ran my fingers across the letters and felt the indentations. I started to open the book, when I heard a thumping on the window.

As I looked up, something flew away from the window. What was that? I looked back down at the book and I heard the thumping again, but still missed its source. It must have been a bird. I looked down again, but this time I looked up quickly and caught the rusty-red cardinal knocking at the window. It was flapping its wings and using its orange beak to tap on the glass.

I stood and went to the window. I could see the marks it left behind. What did it want? I stood there waiting for it to come back and there it was. It seemed like it wanted to tell me something. It flew toward a tall oak tree out in the field. Then it flew back to the window and knocked on it. The cardinal did this over and over. What was this bird trying to show me? I grabbed the heavy book and walked toward the door, when I heard a voice say, "Stop right there!"

I froze. Had I been caught doing nothing? Was I going to get spanked? I turned to face the voice that spoke firmly again: "You have to check that book out if you wish to take it with you."

"Oh, yeah!"

I hadn't even noticed the librarian when I walked in. But here she was, with her lava-colored top bun and heavy bangs that looked like a fresh flow of magma. She wore a white, high-collared shirt, a black pencil skirt, and a gray fitted vest. Over her front left pocket was a name tag that read: MISS JUDGE, LIBRARIAN.

I heaved the tome up onto the high counter. I saw there was a step stool for me to climb on.

Her eyes widened as she looked at the book and then, with an accusing look, asked, "Where did you find this?"

"On the bookshelf," I said.

She let out a bunch of exhausted air and said, "I figured as much, but which shelf? I have been searching for this book for ages!" She looked at me, but this time she really looked at me; her gaze became soft and she covered her mouth. "Oh dear, it's true. … I didn't think I'd be around to see the day, but it must be true."

"What is it? What's true?" I asked.

She seemed anxious as she said, "I can't let you check out this book. It's too important to leave this room. I'm afraid if I let you take it, I'll … I'll never see it again."

She seemed to be thinking a lot and her head looked like it was about to start smoking from all the gears turning so quickly. We were at an impasse.

With what looked to be the solved problem she had been working out in her head, she said, "Tell you what. How about I'll keep it here for you, and you can come read it anytime you want, but just to make sure that it stays safe, we leave it here in the library. How does that sound?"

She seemed genuine, and I felt like I could trust her. So I agreed.

"What's so important about this book?" I asked.

"You don't know? You mean you weren't looking for this book in particular?"

"Not really. It's just the first book I picked up and it looked interesting."

"Wow, just like that." She shook her head in amazement. "You do understand that we ... well, some of us have been searching for years, trying to find this book with all its immensely important information, and you stumble upon it. And the whole time it's been right under our noses. You must be extra special."

"Special?" That is a word that I had never been called, in the good sense. But when she said it, I knew it really meant something. She smiled at me and we made an agreement to keep the book in the library for safekeeping.

I looked toward the window and saw that the bird was still flying back and forth, tapping on the window. I was still curious about what that bird wanted, so I started to leave the library. Miss Judge got up and came around the desk. She opened the door for me and, with a warm smile, she sent me on my way. I promised to return soon. As I walked away, I heard the door close and lock.

CHAPTER 27
THE CLIMBING TREE

On my way out, the two jerks, Thistle and Nettle, came up behind me. As usual with them, something only they thought was funny was making them snicker.

Thistle said, "Hey, Holly, do you need a licensth to look that ugly?"

Their dislike for me must have been the bond that cemented their friendship.

Nettle chimed in, "Hey, Holly, do you still love nature, despite what it did to you? 'Cuz you are ugly."

I already knew that I wasn't the cutest girl in the world. I tried to ignore them and kept walking—until I felt my head lurch back as my body was shoved forward. The hillbilly pushed the bucktoothed girl into me, and I jerked as my head rolled back. It came from out of nowhere. I had never experienced whiplash, but this must be close to what it feels like. I hadn't instigated a thing.

When I turned around, I could see all the way down bucktooth's wide mouth as she gloated at her assault. I wasn't sure what to do, so I stood my ground. I imagined pushing both of them so hard that they flew into the wall, crashing through it as their bodies squirmed in the air, attempting to elude their imminent fall, when mean old Mr. Meanor showed up. He grabbed their arms and escorted them away. As he had them in his firm grip, their once demonic expressions turned into scared puppies with their tails between their legs. It's funny how bullies turn into babies when someone bigger intervenes.

I felt a flood of relief and anger. I decided at that moment, I had to do something to make them stop for good. I wasn't sure what, but I would think of something.

I started to get heated up in my plans to put an end to their constant antagonizing. As I made my way downstairs, I karate-chopped the railings and the walls, inflicting major blows to my invisible assailants. "Hi-yah!" I even attempted to kick them, but when my foot went higher than it should have, I might have pulled a muscle. I limped the rest of the way. I reserved those angry thoughts for later; and the fresh air blew them away when I opened the door to the outside.

* * *

I stepped out onto the lush green grass and looked around in the blue, puffy cloud–filled sky. Where was that rusty orange–beaked cardinal? I went around the building and found the windows that I had seen in the library. I heard the kids playing on the other side of the huge field. Then I noticed the bird pecking at the window. There it was! I was ready to follow it. It flew again to the large oak tree. I ran over to the tree and—you should know, I am a big-time tree climber—and this tree was the most amazing climbing tree I have ever seen. It had a wide, low trunk that split into four sections. From each section, the tree split into four more sections, and each of those split into four more, all the way to the top canopy, which was so thick with leaves, if you fell out of the sky you would bounce on the top. It was a beautiful tree, and I climbed it with all my energy, which seemed to be fueled with pent-up aggravation caused by those two numbskulls. I climbed so high that I forgot that I was looking for the bird, which was now not to be found. Suddenly I realized how high I was and I got scared.

Climbing up is the easy part; getting back down is more challenging. I decided to sit tight for a while. The winds that blew announced their arrival well before actually breezing by me. It was like a wave building momentum, ending with an all-encompassing feeling of fresh air teasing each leaf and strand of hair as the air current passed. I could see beyond the gates of The Children's Horrible House. I had thought we were out in the boonies and by the looks of things, I wasn't wrong.

I thought about escaping, but wasn't sure how, when something caught my eye. It was on the ground and it looked like a small concrete building that was rounded on top. It had pillars on each side and a large door. I thought maybe it was a garden shed, because it was in the middle of a beautiful giant circular garden, but it was too pretty. The rounded garden was filled with colorful flowering trees and exotic-looking plants. It was split in quarters, with pathways that led to an outer rim of mazes bordering the whole garden. If I had seen it from the ground, I would not have noticed its intricate structure. It looked so peaceful, so enchanting.

The wind was coming back again; I could hear it in the distance. This gust was stronger than the others. The leaves on the trees shook as the breeze came rushing through. My eyes closed as I breathed in the light summer-scented air. I lost my bearings for a second and felt disoriented when I opened my eyes. My left eye swallowed a tiny gnat. I rubbed it and blinked a couple times, trying to either set it free or let it drown, but it didn't want to do either.

I started to climb back down when I noticed some ants. Oh no, not those! I knew all too well what they were capable of doing. I wanted to get down faster now. I saw more ants, and bigger ones too. I felt them crawling on my legs and arms and I began to panic.

I cried out in a not very audible voice: "Help!"

The fear seemed to tighten the muscles of my vocal cords, making my voice sound faint. Help!" I called out again.

No one was around to hear me.

Off in the distance I could hear people laughing. They must be laughing at me, stuck in this tree like a scared kitten. I tried to be brave, so I climbed down … but now I came to a huge gap between the limbs. I stretched down my shaking leg, but couldn't quite reach the next branch, when I saw Coriander.

"Coriander," I called down. "Hey! Can you help me?"

He looked around.

"Up here!" I shook the branches.

"Oh, there you are," he said as his hair waved in the wind.

"Yes, here I am. Can you help me?"

"How?"

"Can you go find a ladder?"

"I'll try." He ran off.

As he went, an ant stung me. "Ouch!" I fluttered my hands around my body, trying to get the remaining ants off, but I lost my balance and then, WHAM! I hit the ground back first.

My breath left my body like a whoopee cushion, only not as

amusing. I was a goner, I thought, until I started gasping and gulping like a goldfish out of water.

Coriander's head eclipsed the sun as he bent over my fallen body. "You okay?" he asked. He looked worried. "How many fingers am I holding up?"

I must have blacked out, because next thing I knew I was lying on a couch is Miss Treetment's office. Her back was turned to me as she prepared something. When she turned around, I imagined my mom's face as she smiled and handed me a bowl of ice cream. I started to sit up, but she told me to lie back down. Everything was fuzzy, so I blinked to try to clear my vision. When I rubbed my eyes, I noticed my glasses were gone. I patted my uniform pockets, looking for them.

"I have your glasses," Coriander said reassuringly. He placed them on my face and ruefully smiled.

I smiled too. "Thanks."

"Don't thank me. It's my fault that you fell. I'm really sorry, Holly." He sounded upset.

"It's not your fault. I should have been more careful."

"You got the wind knocked out of you."

Miss Treetment said, "You're lucky you didn't get a concussion. Nothing that a little ice cream can't fix." She gave me a pat on the back and then went back to whatever it was that she did.

I took a bite of ice cream and, *WOW*, it really did make me feel better. I ate it slowly because I wanted the feeling to last as long as possible. I remembered my sisters, Juniper and Ginger, having ice cream–eating contests and my sister Ginger would race to beat Juniper. When Ginger would "win," Juniper would congratulate her while slowly licking each bite, making exaggerated, pleasurable, slurping sounds to let Ginger know who was in fact the real winner.

I looked at Coriander and realized this was the first time I had seen him since we had arrived. "Where have you been this whole time, Coriander?"

"Oh. ... You know, here and there. I've seen you around, but I've been trying to keep to myself. Don't want any trouble; just want to do my time and not cause any fuss."

"You sound like this is jail," I said.

"Isn't it?"

CHAPTER 28
The North Star Estate

Things were running well at The Hawthorne House for Children because of the excellent, carefully picked staff, but mostly because of Reed Trustworthy's acute attention to the balance of making sure the children who came to The Hawthorne House for Children learned why they came and what they needed to do in order to graduate and return home. He believed that proper balance was the key to making children *want* to be obedient.

One day, Saffron Radiant Star returned home. She was older in years but not in maturity. As she entered the grand foyer, a lady she didn't recognize asked her for identification. Saffron was stunned. Some old lady had the nerve to ask *HER* for identification?

"Iris, is it?" She looked at the desktop nameplate. "This is my house. I don't need identification to come into *MY HOUSE!* Okay?" She huffed past this momentary interruption and waltzed right through the entry and headed up to her father's study, ready to grab another pile of money; oh, and maybe say hi to him as well.

Along the way, she noticed a lot of children roaming around

and her former household staff was leading them to different areas of her home.

"What are all these horrible children doing in my home?" She shuddered at the sight. Saffron had no younger siblings and she never wanted any, either. When she had been exposed to little kids, she didn't care for them.

She opened the doors to her father's study, which now had a sign on the door which read: **H. N. Star Library**.

When she entered the room, her father wasn't behind his desk; Reed, the butler, was sitting there … acting like it was *his* study. Who did he think he was? This was her house!

"Where is my father?" she demanded, while looking around for him.

Reed cleared his throat. She was losing her patience.

"WHERE IS MY FATHER?" Her face flared red, exploding like a mushroom bomb.

"He died."

Her face continued to smolder, but the words he spoke started to permeate, causing the fire to fizzle. She blinked in disbelief. It couldn't be, she thought. She wasn't expecting this as her welcome, but her brain began to calculate all the money she was set to inherit; this could still work out.

"Whom do I need to speak with about my inheritance?" she asked.

Reed hesitated again, but answered quicker this time. "You have no inheritance."

At first he had some sympathy for her, but seeing how all she cared about was money, he too became callous. He was hoping that her time away had helped her turn from her selfish, destructive ways; however, he was gravely disappointed.

"What do you mean, I have no inheritance? You think I believe *you*? You probably stole it all, you worthless piece of trash," she yelled in a hissy voice. "Where is my money?"

"Maybe you should ask the state," he roared back.

"What state?" She was confused.

"This state. Your father left *HIS* house, *HIS* estate, and *HIS* money to pay for the running of *THIS* house to the state. This is now a state-run reform house called The Hawthorne House for Children."

"More like The Children's Horrible House! What have you done with this place? It looks awful, with all these horrible children running around and … and all these menial laborers littering my beautiful home. Get them out of here!" She punctuated that sentence with a screech that practically broke the leaded windows of the library.

"They won't be going anywhere, but *you* should leave," Reed emphatically informed her.

"Me, leave? You're hilarious. Why would I leave? This is my house!" she repeated.

"Not anymore. When you disappeared," he informed her, "your father's heart broke into a million unfixable pieces. He blamed himself for your leaving. He knew he should have disciplined you. You took advantage of his kindness and the grief he was suffering from losing his wife …"

"You mean my mother?"

"Yes."

The little sympathy Reed had for her showed up for a brief second as he realized what she had been through as a young child.

"He thought you were dead, Saffron." He called her by her name and somehow it made her less execrable. He cleared his throat and looked into her eyes. "He built the garden you planned for him, you know; and his body is now in the center of it." He motioned for her to look out the window.

CHAPTER 29
THE CHILDREN'S HORRIBLE HOUSE
A VEGETATIVE, NOT ORNAMENTAL GARDEN

After weeks of practice, I thought I was getting pretty good at making beds; I was sure I'd be able to go home soon. There was something that kept me here, though. I realized that I looked forward to class time. I really enjoyed learning about each of the subjects, which was a big difference from my school at home. I really liked all the teachers, but Miss Spelling had a way of making these complicated and complex problems seem tangible. I felt like I was actually learning.

We went outside to one of the gardens. It was on the east side of The Children's Horrible House. There was a big difference between this garden and the one with the building in the center of it. This garden was not "ornamental," as she said, it was "vegetative." It wasn't just a garden that grew one kind of crop, either. It grew them all in different sections. Miss Spelling explained that this type of gardening kept the soil healthy, by having a variety of plants that each cross-fed one another. She also showed us how to weed and prune.

As she was demonstrating the proper procedures, she told us, "The process that you are going through here at The Children's Horrible House, the disciplines you are learning, are very similar to growing a healthy garden. Here, you are learning to weed out bad behavior. And cutting off areas of damaged growth that could lead to bad fruit."

At the time of her explanations and teaching, I really just heard the words, but later on, it began to make sense. She had us look up to the sky and informed us how dependent we are on the weather for sun and rain. That we need both and not too much or too little of each.

"With too much sun, the plants would shrivel up and die. And with too much rain the plants would drown and die. That is why there is a balance, and we are here to learn and appreciate that balance," she informed us.

"The moon is a farmer's best friend. It is best to plant during the full moon and harvest during the new moon. Believe it or not, the moon directly affects our tides and the moisture levels in soil. When the moon is full, the ground has more moisture, which helps nurture new plant growth. And when the soil is dryer, during the waning moon, it is easier to harvest."

After class that day, I caught up to Clover and Cherry. They were walking so closely that I couldn't even see a tiny gap between them. I was excited about what we had learned and wanted to ask them what they thought.

"Wasn't it cool how Miss Spelling explained the relationship between our plants and things in outer space?" I asked.

Clover smiled and started to answer me, but Cherry interjected and said, "We're busy right now; can we ignore you later?"

That stung a bit after I realized her hurtful words were directed at me. I thought about walking away, but instead, I asked Cherry, "Did I do something to you to make you not like me?"

"No," she said. "Actually, yes. You existed," she said dismissively.

Clover didn't seem happy that Cherry was being so mean, but she didn't say anything to stop her, either. I stopped walking with them, but as they continued, Clover stopped walking with Cherry too.

CHAPTER 30
SILENCE

Every night was getting predictable. It was the same crying, but not tonight. I was woken up, but this time by the silence. This should have made me feel good, but instead it seemed like something was wrong. I got up and when I went out into the hallway, Staniel, Danley, and Clover were all there, too. They were discussing something that I must have interrupted as I showed up, because their mouths stayed open, but became silent.

"What's going on? What are you guys doing?" I asked.

"Well, we thought about going to **THE DUNGEON** because every other night we hear crying, but tonight, it's weirdly quiet," Staniel said.

"We wanted to wake you, but didn't have to because you're here already," Clover said. "I guess the silence woke us all up."

I decided to appreciate the fact that Clover was here and didn't mention what had happened earlier.

"Let's go!" I motioned for them all to head to **THE DUNGEON**.

When we got down there, the door stood wide open.

"Why is the door open?" I inquired.

"That explains why there is no crying coming from here," Danley said.

"Yeah … it's empty, except for that stench." Staniel plugged his nose and started to turn away. Danley started to follow him, but I wasn't finished looking around.

"Wait!" I whispered loudly. I examined the room from the hall. "We are going in. We didn't come this far to not go in."

I wasn't going to be scared tonight. None of us really wanted to go in, but we just had to. It was empty and it was a dungeon. It was dark and damp and it smelled like horse manure. I hadn't seen any horses here, but I was familiar with the scent.

Back at my house, we had three horses and two ponies. The horses were Chugger, Sundance, and Dobbin, and the ponies were Licorice and Phoebe. Phoebe was mine. My parents bought her from a door-to-door pony salesman. A couple days after one Christmas, a gentleman wearing suspenders and a hat had pulled up in a cart. The ponies' heads were poking out the sides of the cart. He introduced himself as Mr. Barnaby Stables, and gave my parents a deal they couldn't refuse.

I loved Phoebe. She was so pretty, mostly all black with a few bits of grey and white, always so patient; but you had to be careful because she would kick you if you were in her blind spot. And like all horses and ponies, she had smelly manure.

"What the heck?" I said with much chagrin. I had imagined something much different behind the closed door of THE DUNGEON. But I guess I shouldn't have, considering it was a dungeon.

There wasn't a whole lot to see. It was a dark room with four walls. Clover and I walked up to the walls, and upon closer inspection we were able to make out some drawings and writings. We could see some stick figures getting spanked, and in speech bubbles were the words, "NO! Please don't spank us!"

"Look at this picture. … Who do you think that is?" Danley asked.

A lady with a speech bubble said, "Let me tell you!" She looked stern, but in her overly-embellished teeth was the easy-to-pick-out glob of spinach.

"Um, I'm guessing that's Director Pankins. I wonder who drew these?" Staniel said, and chuckled.

Other than the sparse comical drawings, the room was vacant and not exciting.

✳ ✳ ✳

As we were walking toward our rooms, I looked out of the hallway windows, into the field with the big oak tree. A figure of a woman in a long, white, flowing dress glided through the garden and into the garden shed. The hair on my arms stood up.

"Did you see that?" I asked.

They did.

It was a ghost!

It was a lady ghost and we all saw it.

If any of us had been alone, we probably would have gone back to our rooms, scared as kittens. But tonight, with the four of us together and a steadfast determination, we were brave—until we heard footsteps headed in our direction.

Our bodies tensed and then Clover ran. Staniel and Danley looked at each other and then at me. I took off and followed Clover. She was a fast runner, I had learned, but the PP twins were faster.

✳ 117 ✳

They blew past us like a bullet train. I tried to keep up, but I wasn't used to running long distances. I willed my legs to keep running. Clover was staying at my pace. Wondering whose footsteps were coming after us propelled me to run faster, even though I was exhausted.

When we made it outside, we were gasping for breath. It seemed we were out of danger. We were hiding behind some thick bushes.

After a couple minutes, our breathing steadied and Danley spoke up. "Who do you think that was?"

"Probably Major Whoopins or mean old Mr. Meanor," I said, grateful that we were not discovered.

"Maybe it was Mr. Ree … but who knows?" Staniel asked.

"Where do you think the ghost went?" Clover asked, looking around.

I scanned the area, too. A mist blanketed the ground. The grass stood soft with nighttime dew. The half-moon shone brightly and the big billowy clouds provided even more reflective light.

"Let's check in the garden." I waved for them to come along.

We crept silently toward the garden encircled by overgrown ivy. We came up to a stone-and-iron gate. In the center of the gate was a circle with two intersecting lines running vertically and horizontally through the middle of it. I touched the cold metal symbol and hesitantly opened the huge gate, and stepped inside. Wall-like shrubs led to another long pathway of shrubs as we followed the trail.

I felt like I was absent from my normal hesitant body. I was brave, but still reluctant; maybe my nerves were on alert. My body was having an internal battle. As I turned around and looked at Clover, she met me with a reassuring smile. Having my friends with me must have propelled my normally hesitant self with much-needed assurance. Staniel and Danley marched with the same dualistic rhythm. We finally came to the real threshold. The maze that we had bravely charged through was behind us, and we were looking into the hidden mystical garden within the maze. We ducked down under the drooping honeysuckle vines and stepped inside.

"Whoa, this is cool!" Staniel whispered as he slowly stood up straight.

I silently nodded in agreement.

The garden opened up to a most enchanting habitat. Backlit by the moon was a giant weeping willow that seemed to glimmer as it dipped its dripping foliage into the natural-looking pond that reflected the ethereal glowing tree as if it were one single double image: one right side up, the other upside down. Fireflies danced around in the air like winged phosphorescent dragons. I wished I could paint, but I knew I would never be able to capture the beauty of this magnificent glowing garden better than seeing it with my eyes in this moment.

A barely audible buzz sounded like tiny fairies flickering from grass blades to luminescent mushroom caps, in everlasting rhythms. I bent down and brushed my fingers through the short piles of grass that carpeted the ground in soft luxury. With each sweep, the grass reflected different shades of shimmering green.

"Check out this tree! It looks like it's covered in ice cream cones!" Danley was standing near a very tall tree while he held one of the conical blooms in his hands and sniffed deeply. "It smells good, but not like ice cream, that's for sure." He dipped his nose in again.

We all smelled them. The tree was covered in them and, on closer inspection, the flowers were actually clusters of little blossoms that looked like tiny snapdragons. In the moonlight, it was hard to see the exact colors, but they looked mostly white, with pink and yellow dots.

"Look over there!" Clover ran to a hugely-trunked and strong-branched tree and hopped into a natural hanging swing that was waiting to be ridden. This tree had roots that seemed to reach from the branches, into the ground, making the tree so wide that it even had arches of rooms within the base. I peeked inside one and imagined gnomes making cozy woodland dens.

"Wheeeeee! Wheeeeee!" Clover swung back and forth, higher and higher.

"How did this get here?" I wondered aloud. It was as if the swing was made out of the garden and it grew from this tree. The vines which held the thick, green, mossy seat were braided with what looked like corn silk.

The twins began to swing from the vines that looked like they were developing into new swings. They made Tarzan noises as they swayed from vine to vine. I grabbed one too, and flew along with them. My fears vanished as I swung in the bright, glowing greenness that surrounded me. We swung until we were weary, and we landed in a thick pallet of soft grass.

The twins wanted to explore more, and I followed. This had to be the biggest garden I had ever seen. Perhaps the outer circular shape made it seem as if it could go on eternally. Clover kept swinging for a bit, and then she jumped off mid-swing and came along. As we walked, we noticed these glowing, fog-filled orbs that were suspended by different lengths of invisible string. I tried to walk up to them to hold them, but the closer I got, the farther they went from me, always just out of reach.

"What are these?" Staniel asked as he, too, tried to grab one.

"Maybe they are spirits trapped in a bubble," Clover said.

"Could be. Whatever they are, they're cool. I wish I could grab one and pop it, to see what's inside," Danley said.

"Maybe that's why you can't reach them. You might kill 'em if you pop 'em," Clover said.

"I don't want to kill 'em!" Danley insisted. "C'mon, let's see what's over there." He pointed to a big stone building covered in dark green creeping fig. The plants and flowers were all perfectly manicured and pruned with such attention to detail. I noticed a vine covered in white blooms that looked like a turbine. They seemed to be moving ever so slowly, but indeed moving.

"Check these out, guys! These flowers are moving!"

"Oh, I know what these are. They're moonflowers, and if we wait, they'll fully open up," Clover excitedly informed us.

We watched them creep open for a while, but then the twins got antsy and walked ahead. Clover and I watched the flowers some more, until they fully opened, breathing on us their perfumed scent. It was worth the wait. The blooms were bigger than my hands and the little yellow pistils poked out in greeting.

After our nighttime show, we walked past sculptures and totem poles that watched over the plants and guarded them. An enormous stone ball appeared to be resting on top of a pyramid. Through the center of the sphere, a gurgling fountain glazed over it and fell in tiny drops into a pond scattered with water lilies and orange and white fish. We walked over a stone bridge and then under an arbor that was blooming with giant purple-faced flowers.

"Wow, look at this!" I stopped and marveled at this purple-petaled masterpiece that popped out from the vines. "I wonder what it's called."

They shrugged and kept walking. I stared at it for an instant, committing it to memory. I wanted to make sure to ask Miss Spelling.

At the center of the garden was the building that I had seen from the tree from which I had fallen. It wasn't a shed. It was much too fancy. We scampered our way toward the front.

My nose was suddenly filled with a most wonderful scent. It made me want to sniff harder to find the source of this sweet smell. I followed the aroma like a hound dog, to a big bush with small, white, fluted flowers. I dunked my scent-seeking nose inside the blooms, closed my eyes, and breathed in the sweet nectar.

"What are you doing?" Clover asked. "You look like a bumblebee."

"Can't you smell that? It smells so good! I wonder what it is?" I dreamily inquired.

Clover smelled it too, but I guess she wasn't as impressed.

"It's night-blooming jasmine," Danley said.

I stood up and asked, "How did you know that?"

"Just do," Danley said.

I pulled off a stem with a few flowers and tucked it in my pocket to take with me.

"That is the biggest door I have ever seen!" Clover's mouth hung open as she stared at the daunting doorway.

The huge stone door on the front of the dome-shaped structure looked like it couldn't be opened by normal humans. The words carved into the stone read:

Hawthorne North Star
Beloved Husband, Adoring Father
Rest in Peace
Born August 16, 1924 ⸱ Died July 14, 1976

Just out front, in the center, lay fresh flowers arranged in a beautiful bouquet. A loud call for help ricocheted from behind the wall. We all looked at each other, eyes bugging out of our heads. We kneeled down quickly and quietly. Staniel and Danley cupped their hands over their mouths, holding back scared squeals. My lips rolled up my mouth like a retracting bungee. Clover's mouth opened wider than her eyes, which were fully round, exposing a lot of the white parts.

"Whoa! It is a ghost!" Staniel whispered.

"It's the ghost, all right," Danley softly said to his twin.

I covered their mouths, trying to silence them. But when I did, I made a clop sound and they both scolded me by "Gurrrrr"-ing. More calls for help echoed. Then we heard flapping wings descend all around us. Like white-robed angels, a flock of peacocks surrounded us, calling out cries for help. I instantly recognized the sound. This must have been the sounds we had been hearing night after night! I thought it was a woman or a baby crying, but could it have been this muster of peacocks that alarmed us nightly? They didn't seem happy about our presence in their garden. Their tail feathers fanned out, vibrating to fullness. They began to march closer, daring us to challenge them. We instantly surrendered and weaved through their formation.

Staniel and Danley took off first. Clover grabbed my arm as we darted away. I heard the peacocks coming after us! We were running, but somehow we were lost. It seemed like we were running in circles. Where was the way out? The shrubs all looked the same and we kept running into dead ends. We thought we were on the right track as we ran, but when we got to the end, we had nowhere else to go.

I heard a loud whisper: "Psssst! Over here."

I turned to the right and saw Coriander signaling us to follow. We ran after him. He led us around and past the tall trees and flowers. I ran face first into the purple-faced flowery vine which filled my very open mouth. I stopped, spat it out, and brushed off the remaining leaves. Coriander grabbed my arm and led me through the mazed shrubs as we quickly made our way out of the garden. He took us back to the bushes where we had been previously hiding.

"Where? How?" I started to ask, but was too out of breath.

"What are you guys doing?" he demanded to know.

"We think we may have figured out who the crying ghost is," I told him.

"Who is it?" he asked.

"Peacocks," Staniel and Danley blurted.

His eyes rolled in impatience. He turned away and started walking.

"Wait, Coriander. Where are you going?" I asked.

"To bed, which is where you all should go, too."

"What are you, our mom or something?" Staniel asked.

"I'm something," Coriander answered.

"Yeah, you're something, all right," Danley chirped in his raspy fashion.

"Hey," I said, "Coriander, thanks for getting us out of there." I tried to rally the others to thank him as well, by giving them stern looks. Then I thought a second and asked him, "Umm ... what were you doing in the garden?"

"None of your business."

He turned and walked away. As he continued farther, the mist that swam on the ground swallowed him and he disappeared.

I was hurt by his words, but after I thought about it, I don't think he was directing them at me.

Later, when I got back into bed, I was thinking about the peacocks. Were they really the source of all those cries? How did it sound like the cries were coming from **THE DUNGEON**? What were they doing in the garden? Were they guarding Hawthorne North Star's tomb? The ghost in the white, flowing dress emerged from my memory. So, maybe the peacocks explained the cries I had heard, but they didn't account for the ghost sighting. Then I thought about Coriander. I was wondering how he was always around at just the right time. It was like he was a guardian angel or something. He was with me on the bus ride here, he helped me after I fell out of the tree, and he guided us through the garden maze. Maybe he had a super power?

CHAPTER 31
The North Star Estate

Saffron turned and walked over to the window. Reed pointed to the right so she could see the garden below and the domed building in the center of it. She recognized the circular maze she had planned to encompass the whole garden, and the tall chestnut trees that were in full bloom. The weeping willow's drooping limbs humbly asked for her presence. She felt drawn to the garden like a force stronger than any magnetic attraction.

She ran out of the house toward the tall oak tree and the garden. As she continued, her hand grazed the tree like she was touching an old friend. She went through the tall walls of the maze and found her way to the garden entrance, and followed the pathway toward the mausoleum. A couple of white peacocks were proudly stalking around the perimeter, but they didn't seem interested in her.

Right beside the building were her favorite plants: lavender, lemongrass, and jasmine. She knew her father had planted them for her. The garden was even more grand in person. Seeing it in full dimension was a feeling she had never felt before. Was it accomplishment? Was it pride? It was bigger than those words. She couldn't name it, but she felt it.

She planted herself within the comforting foliage and thought back to when her mother used to take her out at night to stargaze. One night they saw a series of shooting stars. Her mother told her of her people's belief that shooting stars were a bad omen, that they were a sign of a person's soul going into the afterlife or an approaching death. Her mother became scared for her people. She grabbed the night-blooming jasmine and crushed it, and burned it to ward off any evil spirits that were coming to take away her loved ones. Sings-in-the-Meadow recalled her people's prayers and sang them to the listening spirits. Whenever Saffron smelled night-blooming jasmine, she thought of her mother and she felt protected from evil. She bent over as she felt a wave of grief overcome her. She had no one. She was homeless. She was broken. ... She broke down ... and wept.

Darkness had fallen by the time her grief subsided. She got up and wondered where she would go. She had no money, no transportation, and no hope. As she walked, she tried to think about what she could do to support herself, now that she was on her own. She really had no notable skills, no personal goals, no unfulfilled dreams, no home or family. She heard a train whistle in the distance. She thought about jumping in front of it and ending her miserable life. It actually seemed like her best option. She started to stride toward it with a purpose. "Great," she said, "the one purpose I've ever felt compelled to do is end my life," she said, sarcastically berating herself.

The train was slowly huffing and puffing at a speed that, if she ran really fast, she could catch. Her mind was blurring her purpose. Was she catching the train to go somewhere, or was she jumping in front of it? Her mind started to go in circles and she panicked.

She didn't know what to do, so she ran and ran as fast as she could, hoping her mind would catch up with her body, which was now making her decisions. She caught up with the train.

CHAPTER 32
THE CHILDREN'S HORRIBLE HOUSE
THE KEY

I was making the beds like a robot today. My mind was elsewhere. When I was finishing up and giving this bed the final tucks, my hand felt something underneath the mattress. It had the tactile property of metal. I popped my head under the mattress and saw a key. A really old-looking key. It was big too. It had a really odd shape. I had seen this kind of key before, but not one this ornate and mysterious looking. My dad is a collector of all things antique. He had keys very similar to this. I wondered what door this opened. Was this the key to **THE DUNGEON**? Or maybe it was the key to Director Pankins' office. It looked important, but why would it be under this bed? Who would leave it there?

These were the questions I asked Clover and the PP twins at lunch that day. They were just as curious as I was. We were passing it around when Coriander came up to the table.

"Hi, Coriander. Pull up a seat and join us," I said.

He seemed hesitant.

"Look what I found!" I tried to entice him and it worked. He took it, examined it, and asked where I found it.

I spoke up proudly. "I found it under a mattress of a bed that I was making in one of the fancier rooms. What do you think it unlocks?" I asked.

"Well, it's a skeleton key, so maybe it unlocks a coffin," he said sarcastically ... at first. It seemed as if a light came on inside Coriander's brain. His face reflected the connecting of the dots almost in slow motion. "You guys, I think I know what this is," he whispered, "but I need to be sure. Supposedly there is a book hidden within The Children's Horrible House that tells where the fortune of Hawthorne North Star is hidden. This may be the key that unlocks the treasure." His whispers were getting louder and more excited.

I was so happy that I was the source of his excitement. Okay, maybe it wasn't me, and it was really the key that excited him, but I was the one who found it, after all. Then, in a rush of beautiful brain activities, a certain word that he had spoken jumped out of my brain. BOOK!

"Did you say there was a book that you were looking for? I think I know where it is," I proudly announced.

"No way," Coriander said in disbelief.

"Yup, at least I think so."

"Where did you find it?" he asked.

"In the library."

"That's a strange place to find a book," Danley said in a goofy tone.

Coriander rolled his eyes, tilted his head, and said in an unsure voice, "We don't know if it's the right book, now, do we? It would be way too obvious of a place to hide a book. I can't imagine it would be that easy." He seemed unsure and pessimistic.

I told them about my encounter with Miss Judge and how she was going to hold the book for me.

"Are you kidding?" Coriander seemed annoyed. "Of course she will hold it for you. Now we'll never see it again. I bet you anything she will have accidentally 'misplaced it.' " His hands accentuated "misplaced it" in air quotes.

"Let's go now. Let's go to the library and see." I was ready.

We cleared our plates and marched off to claim our property. Actually, it wasn't our property, but you know … we were on a mission.

When we got to the library, the doors were locked. I shook the doors in annoyance.

"Aw, man! Now what?" Clover stomped.

That mean old Mr. Meanor seemed to appear out of nowhere. "What seems to be the problem?" he croaked.

We straightened up and tried to act as properly as we knew how, but it didn't seem to have any effect on him.

"I'm waiting for an answer," he said in a warning tone.

I thought that since so far we had had a decent relationship, maybe I should be the one to do the explaining. Clover must have thought the same thing. Before I could get out any words, she was explaining how we were wanting to further our education by engaging in great works of literature.

Mr. Meanor wasn't buying it and said simply, "Library's closed."

"Why?" I asked.

I guess you weren't supposed to ask "why" to mean old Mr. Meanor. I guess you were supposed to do what he said to do, because now I was on my way to THE DUNGEON. I didn't even have time to look back at my friends.

Have you ever wished you had no voice? Or wished you couldn't talk? Or wished you could go back in time and not say something stupid? I was wishing all that so hard right now. I had never been in so much trouble as I was sure I was in for. I was terrified of THE DUNGEON. What was going to happen to me? Were they going to spank me super hard? Were they going to yell at me? Who was going to yell at me? Was it going to be Mr. Meanor? Or Director Pankins?

Mr. Meanor was whipping me around the hallways. I felt like I was on death row, about to be a goner—no trial, no judgment, just a goner.

When we got to THE DUNGEON, Mr. Meanor handed me off to Major Whoopins, who looked disturbed at seeing me here. Mean old Mr. Meanor waited inside while the door shut loudly behind us. I stood silently with my back against the wall, hoping to hide the target that had to be on my backside. My hands were crossed behind my back, giving extra protection to shield it. Director Pankins appeared from the back door that until now I hadn't known existed.

"Whom do we have here?" she sneered.

In his croaky voice, Mr. Meanor explained, in detail, the crime I had committed as she listened hungrily.

I found the manure scent source! In the room which Director Pankins had just exited, bags labeled PLANT FERTILIZER / MANURE were stacked in piles next to wheelbarrows and other gardening tools. So it *was* the butt of The Children's Horrible House, I realized, with weird relief at figuring out at least one thing about this place.

"Mr. Meanor, thank you, you are dismissed," Director Pankins informed him.

He shuffled his heels around and left the room.

CHAPTER 33
THE OBVIOUS ANSWER

"Why? … Why? Why?" she asked in varying tones. "You ask why? … That's a good question."

I was confused. I thought I was in trouble and now it seemed that my crime was good?

"Why are you here? Why is anybody here? *Why am I here*?" she turned and yelled dramatically.

So I guess it wasn't a good question. This must be one of those times when grownups are being sensationally sarcastic. I should be good at this stuff.

My sister, Ginger, was voted most sarcastic of her class. When I tried to impress her with one of my epiphanies, she'd roll her eyes and say, "Hey, Sphincter (she loved to call me this), here's a quarter. Why don't you call someone who cares. Just make sure you bring me back the change." Or if I asked where something was, she'd tell me it was up my butt. Somehow I always believed everyone … that's why people called me gullible. And I believed them, too.

Director Pankins stood there and stared at me. If she wasn't so intimidating, I would have thought she was pretty. She had a natural earthly beauty, similar to the lady in the portrait in her office. But Director Pankins had devious eyes when she drilled them into your soul. It was like she was trying to extricate information from me telepathically. Maybe she wanted me to answer her.

I thought about it a second, looked at Major Whoopins, and answered her with the first thing that came to mind. "Because none of us made our beds and cleaned our rooms?"

This obvious statement seemed to confuse Director Pankins. She laughed, started to utter what could be words, and then she smiled. "You know, in all my years here, no one has ever answered that question so bluntly. And in all honesty, I have to say … yes! That is why. That is why you are here, why everyone else is here and why …"

The rest of her sentence must have fallen off a cliff, never to be uttered. She hung her head and looked down. I followed her gaze and noticed the toilet paper that was stuck to the bottom of her shoe. Her head tilted and out of her left eye, she tried to sneak to see if I had noticed the paper. I couldn't hide the knowledge on my face. She kicked her foot around trying to loosen the paper. Eventually Major Whoopins put out his hand, stopping her uncoordinated jig, and pulled the paper free from her high-heeled shoe. She composed herself as best she could, but I could tell she was about to blow a fuse.

"You know what?" she asked. "I think you need to learn a lesson here."

Don't step on toilet paper? is what ran through my brain and lucky for me it didn't run out of my mouth.

"I think you need to write some sentences. Five hundred times, you will write, 'I am at The Children's Horrible House because I would not make my bed or clean my room.' Is that understood?" She looked back at Major Whoopins, who shrugged his shoulders in agreement.

"Yes, ma'am."

"Instead of your free day this Sunday, you will be completing this assignment in the library. Understood?"

"Yes, ma'am!" *Am I lucky or what?* I tried not to sound too excited. "Yes, ma'am," I said, this time much more forlornly.

My punishment was not so bad. All I can say is that I would much rather write a million sentences in the library than get the paddle from Major Whoopins, or any of the other punishments they utilized here. Plus, I would be able to find the book Coriander was so curious about. It seemed that my hardships might be taking a new turn. I might be able to figure out the mystery that loomed around this paradoxical dwelling.

CHAPTER 34
STAR DAY

There was a mind-blowing breakthrough in class today. I was very glad for it because it took my attention away from Cherry and Clover looking like they were in their own fun world. Cherry glanced over at me and stuck out her tongue. What was that for? I know this may seem crazy, but it actually hurt and it made me want to stick my tongue out at her in retaliation. I waited for her to look back, but it was like she wouldn't look over at me on purpose. How was I going to get her back if she wouldn't even look at me? I got bored with my futile thoughts and tuned in to the teacher.

Miss Gyde told us about a fantastic celestial conjunction coming on the horizon. I had never cared about learning or school, but it was like a light came on in my head that was now forever illuminated. My curiosity was limitless, as well as the questions that followed the lesson.

She told us about the Star of Panivita. Even the name sounded phenomenal.

"The Star of Panivita is actually the conjunction of the planets Jupiter, Venus, and also the star Regulus. On the night of our Star

Day Celebration these three celestial bodies will appear to become one very bright star in our eastern night sky," she explained as she was drawing a picture on the blackboard.

I shot my hand up into the air and waved it around.

Miss Gyde called on me. "Holly, do you have a question?"

"Yes, Miss Gyde, what is Star Day?"

She set down her chalk and said, "Oh, well, it is an annual celebration we have to honor Hawthorne North Star, the founder of The Children's Horrible House. He was a great man; some say he was a savior for all the children who have gone astray. His birthday happens to coincide with some amazing celestial events."

I recalled the date on the building, August 16. I remembered because it was just two days before my own.

"See here, children." She walked over to her pull-down study guides and she pointed to an image of our solar system. "Jupiter will be the brightest and Venus will be the second brightest. Actually, they are very far apart in outer space, but to us here on Earth, they will appear to be almost one giant star." She stopped talking and finished drawing it on the chalkboard.

I had seen pictures of this star in some books at home, but had never paid much attention. I didn't think it really existed.

"On Star Day," she said, "the two planets will be joined by Regulus and the full moon, also called the Green Corn Moon by Native Americans. They called the moon this because it was almost time for the harvest and the corn was still green. So, these two planets, Jupiter and Venus, will converge with the star, Regulus, making what is now referred to as Panivita, in a beautiful celestial display toward the east at dusk." She continued her lesson about the ancient understandings of these planets.

"Historically, Jupiter was symbolized as the 'planet of kings' and Venus, a most loving 'mother.' So when these two come together, and then are joined by Regulus, also known as the 'king' star, it meant a royal birth! Guess in which constellation this event took place?" she asked as we were on the edge of our seats waiting to hear the answer.

"Leo! Leo the lion," she said with so much enthusiasm that it rubbed off on us. "But, back to our time. Although conjunctions between Jupiter and Venus of this magnitude are rare, there will be one on Star Day and another that will be even brighter next year. Let's hope for clear weather for our celebration, but mostly so that we might witness this amazing cosmic show."

My brain was excited by its new contents. I was learning a lot here, but it all seemed random. I wondered if there was a connection between all this newfound collective information. Could the book and the amazing garden be related to this lesson? Why did Hawthorne North Star find these subjects so worthy of study and exploration? When I thought about it, it was pretty cool to learn about how small we are in this limitless universe, yet what a big impact we can have on it. Maybe Hawthorne was on to something.

Class had never passed so quickly. I had all this exciting information, but had no idea if I would be able to remember it all when the time came.

* * *

Right after I left Miss Gyde's class, I went to look for Miss Spelling. I found her at her desk, looking over some papers. I wanted to specifically ask her a question.

"Hi, Miss Spelling, do you have a moment?" I asked.

"Of course, dear. How can I assist you?"

"Miss Spelling, I was wondering if you knew what kind of flower this is." I drew it roughly on the chalkboard as I described it to her.

"It's on a vine with big leaves and it has a big green-and-purple face. Oh, and it has all these little petals that poke out from it like a sea urchin." I was actually impressed with my drawing and my description.

She tilted her head and quietly asked me, "Where did you see this flower?"

I didn't know how to answer this and I didn't think about the fact that I saw it in the garden, a place I might not be allowed to enter. I tried to answer quickly.

"It's my mother's favorite and I can't remember the name." I may not have been lying because I was sure that if my mother saw it, it would become *or* it could already be her favorite.

She tilted up just one of her eyebrows and tried to examine my face. Then she smiled and said, "It's a passionflower, and just so happens to be Hawthorne North Star's favorite. He planted it for his beloved." She paused and then said, "You'd better be careful."

CHAPTER 35
THE SECRET

I couldn't wait for Sunday to come. So when it finally did, I woke early and made my bed and set off for the library. As I came to the doors, I noticed the circles with the intersecting lines in the grill. I wondered what they meant and why they were repeated.

I opened the doors and looked around for Miss Judge. I didn't see her right away. With my paper and pencil in hand, I went to the long wooden table. I really wanted to go look for the book, but knew I'd be in trouble if I didn't write my sentences first. I got to work.

Halfway through, though, the library door opened and in walked the PP twins and Clover. They approached the table and sat down.

"What are you guys doing here?" I whispered.

"Looking for you, silly," Clover said, as if stating the obvious.

"You guys might get in trouble," I said.

"Don't worry about us," Danley said. "We are going to look for the book."

They got up and I tried to stop them, but then I remembered that the book wasn't that easy to find for just anyone. So I let them explore. When they came back empty-handed, I gloated a little on the inside.

"Where is it?" Staniel asked.

"I'll look for it as soon as I'm finished with the sentences I have to write."

"Finish those later," the three pleaded.

I was chomping at the bit to find the book too, so I got up and went to the place where I had found it the last time. And sure enough, there it was again. I picked it up and felt the indentations of the title, "*Sage Themes*." There had to be a hidden message in the pages of this book. It looked like such an important book, bound in heavy leather and golden letters. The more I looked at the front cover, an image I hadn't noticed before revealed itself. At the center of the top of the book was a circular cross, like the ones on the library doors and garden gate. Raised bands went to each of the four corners, where a perfectly formed passionflower poked out of the leather. A domed building was surrounded by a garden. I looked at one of the plants in particular, and then recognized the fluted blooms of the night-blooming jasmine. It was placed in the exact same location in the real garden. And now it was obvious what building this was … the tomb of Hawthorne North Star. The three of us stared in amazement. I carefully opened the heavy cover and noticed the quote that began the book:

> Whatever good thing each one does,
> This he will receive back.

Here it was again. "I saw this above the fireplace in D-Hall," I said.

"Yeah, we noticed it too," one of the twins said.

"I wonder what it means?" Clover questioned. "Maybe it's kind of like karma?"

"What's karma?" the twins asked simultaneously.

Clover tilted her head to the side and squinted, her eyes trying to form the words of her response. "Basically, it's you get what you give." She punctuated her explanation with a quick single nod.

The twins seemed satisfied with her definition. It worked for me as well. As we looked carefully through the rest of the pages, we noted that it was filled with carefully drawn pictures identifying different species of plants. It described the proper times to plant certain crops and vegetables. The varying times were completely dependent on lunar cycles. Plant this when the moon is full. Harvest this with the new moon.

"Look, it's just like what we learned in Miss Spelling's class … the soil's dampness seems to be dependent on the tides, which the moon influences." I pointed to a picture in the book.

The precisely drawn pictures corresponded to each description. The book also referenced the constellations and which ones lined up with certain times of the year. And it gave dates on which plants and constellations needed to be in alignment for optimal growth and abundance to occur. There were also formulas in order to figure out all of these things.

But what did this mean? Why was this book so important? I wondered why these subjects were so important and repetitious to this place.

Miss Judge appeared in the midst of our discussions. "Wherever did you find this?"

She bent down and tried to grab the book, but the twins covered it protectively. We were all stunned by her sudden presence. I was sure we were headed for **THE DUNGEON**.

She looked directly at me. "What's your name again? What is it? Molly? No, that's not it," she said, and corrected herself. "Holly? Am I right?"

"Yes, ma'am, that's my name."

"How did you find this? Again?" She looked flabbergasted.

"It was in the same spot as last time," I said.

"Oh no … no … that's not possible!" Miss Judge said in disbelief.

I shifted around uncomfortably, not knowing what to say or do.

She took me by the hand over to her desk, away from the others, and quietly confided in me. "Last time, eh-hem, when you were here last, I put the book in a very secret, I mean safe spot. I wanted to be sure that it wouldn't be lost." Her eyes shifted around to see if anyone was witnessing our conversation.

"When I came back to work the next day, it was gone. I looked everywhere. I could not find it. But you seem to be able to find it with no trouble at all. Tell me, if you would, please, what is your secret?" she implored.

I wasn't sure how to respond, because there was no secret. It simply seemed to be in the right place for me to find. But I knew she wanted me to tell her something much more fantastic. So I made my eyes big and told her, with all seriousness, "I'm special."

Her head swung a bit to the right and her shoulders stood straight as she backed away while her eyes stayed fixed on me. She had already called me special, but I guess at the time she must not have meant it. Her thoughts mirrored her expression as it turned to amazement, and even she began to believe it too … that I was special.

"Will you let me see it?" she asked. "The book. Will you let me help? I might be able to help you decipher some of the true meanings. I mean, I have been educating myself for years, preparing myself for the off chance that I would one day have a firsthand encounter with this incredible book."

We walked back to where we left it. Everyone was gone, including the book. We both became frantic, wondering where the book and everyone went.

"You have to find that book, Holly," Miss Judge said nervously. "It is of utmost importance that you recover that book!"

"I'll go get it now!" I darted for the door.

I felt her urgency and went to look for everyone. I couldn't find them anywhere; it was like they disappeared. I looked outside. I went to the tree, I went to D-Hall, I looked in everyone's room, but found no one.

I put my hands in my pockets in disappointed exhaustion. I felt something hard and small … was it the key? I pulled it out. It was a hairpin. I rubbed it around in my fingers trying to figure out where everyone went … hoping that the rubbing would act like a genie in a bottle, and it would pop out and give me three wishes or even clues as to their location.

Where did I put that key? Then I remembered; Coriander had it. I paced the floors wondering where I should continue my search. I started to walk aimlessly and the longer I walked the madder I became at my friends. Where were they? They better not get me in trouble with all these shenanigans. My footsteps became louder and angrier as I went up the stairs. The walls echoed the breaths that I was purposely huffing in and out.

I walked back up and past the library. At the end of the hall was a small wooden door that I never thought to look at before, but now I was leaving no stone unturned in my search. I stood in front of it, examining whether or not to turn the handle. I twisted the handle and found everyone, including Coriander, who seemed to be waiting for me.

"What's going on? What are you guys doing in here? Why did everyone take off?" I asked, but no answer would be good enough for me right now.

Coriander ignored my questions and went straight to the point. "Listen, Holly, you might be in over your head. There's a lot of stuff you don't know about or understand."

I slumped in exasperation. What he said clicked and it angered me.

"Who are you to tell me what I don't know or understand?" No one ever thought I was smart enough, even Coriander, I guessed.

Coriander grabbed both of my shoulders and gently shook me in order to make his point clear. "You and your friends are meddling in things that you really should ignore."

"I really don't know what you mean. Are you talking about the book that *I* found? … Maybe it's you who doesn't understand." I had him on that one.

"Look, Holly, I'm just trying to protect you," he explained.

"Really? I think you are just as curious as we are and you are trying to figure stuff out too. Look, I'm trying to return this book to Miss Judge, the librarian," I protested. "I'm not meddling. Things are happening to me, and I don't know why."

He looked at me for an extended period, examining the truthfulness in my face. Clover and the twins seemed concerned, but weren't sure how to proceed. I saw Danley holding the heavy book. It looked like they all knew something that I didn't. I walked up to Danley, grabbed the book, and headed back to the library.

"Wait, Holly," they all called.

"Leave me alone," I said as I turned my back and ran.

Coriander followed me. It seemed like he wanted to tell me something, but he was having trouble keeping up. "Wait up! Holly, I need to tell you something!"

I wanted to keep running to get out some frustrations, but the cumbersome book prevented me. I slowed down, and we walked in silence until his mouth could no longer restrict the words from purging.

"Listen, Holly, I know this book has something to do with a mystery that I've been trying to figure out since I got here, but can't figure out how it all goes together. For some reason, you are part of this mystery—in what capacity, I still don't know—but I'm trying to put all the pieces together."

"Honestly, Coriander, I really have no idea what you mean and I'm not happy with you right now." I kept walking.

He stopped me and said, "Maybe it will make more sense if I tell you what I already do know. But we have to go somewhere where no one can find us or hear us."

CHAPTER 36
THE LONG HISTORY

As we were walking toward the library, I started to open the door, but he signaled for me to follow him. Soon we were outside of another ordinary-looking wooden door, but when he tried to open it, it was locked. He wiggled the door trying to get it to open, but nothing.

"Wait a second." I handed him the heavy book. I thought I would give the hairpin a try, just for the heck of it. I unbuttoned my deep pocket and pulled it out, twisted it like I had seen in the movies, and inserted the metal loopy pin into the lock. I turned it to the right and … voilà! It opened.

"Now we know you are a master lock picker," he said, impressed.

"One mystery solved; many more to come." I put the hairpin back in my pocket.

Inside was a dark, steep set of stairs. The carpeted treads were very narrow. As we made our way to the top, the attic opened up to the most cheerful color of yellow imaginable. The yellow walls were wooden tongue-and-groove planks. There was one huge room with little rooms that fed off the big one. At the very end was a room filled with stuffed animals—not the soft, cute, and cuddly kind. These animals were once alive, and now they were stuffed. Next to that was the laundry room. The machines were grinding away like steam engines on a train and the drying racks were walls that glided in and out of pocket doors as big as ping pong tables.

When I came out of the laundry room, Coriander was staring at an enormous framed picture on the back wall. As I went to see what enticed him, I noticed a room off to the right. It had a dormer window at the end. It stepped down about four stairs into the most whimsical room imaginable.

The room itself looked like it was the attic from *The Velveteen Rabbit*, a perfect place for an imagination to bring a stuffed animal to life. The room was the ultimate rumpus room for an overprivileged child. In the center was the biggest dollhouse you could ever imagine. It was a replica of The Children's Horrible House, and it was furnished extravagantly, like a fancy home. It had intricately carved antique furniture and even window dressings. It was like looking at The Children's Horrible House the way it was intended, but from a giant's point of view.

A lot of colorful toys and handmade dolls lined the shelves. I picked up one doll that was different from the rest. It had long, dark hair and was wearing animal skin and black moccasins. I wondered who played with this doll. I wished I could play pretend and imagine the day away with all these magical toys. I didn't have a whole lot of my own toys at my house, and being the youngest of five, I basically got hand-me-down everything.

Coriander said something to take me out of my wishful thinking, so I walked up to see what he was looking at. It was a bunch of names and lines that would connect to another name. The toys looked a lot more interesting.

"This is the Star family tree," he explained. "At the top here are two names: Comfort Lone Star, who was married to Viburnum Rose Bush—Hawthorne's mother and father." Below their names was a line that pointed to Hawthorne North Star and another line that connected to Oleander Bright Star.

"Hawthorne had a brother named Oleander Bright Star, it looks like." Coriander was reading and thinking out loud.

"Look. Here's his wife, beside Hawthorne's name, Hyacinth Split Peabody. She died at around thirty years of age, it seems." He calculated her age in his head. "But not before they had had four children: Hawthorne North Star Jr., Fern Wandering Star, Vine Twinkling Star, and Willow Faint Star."

"I like their names," I said. "They're all unique."

"Strange," Coriander said.

"Strange to you, maybe, but I think they are cool."

"No, I'm not talking about the names," he said. "I'm talking about this." He pointed to another line.

"This line, for what would be another spouse, was left empty." He pondered. "Although, it shows the product of that union, named Saffron Radiant Star. Meaning, Hawthorne plus blank had a child named Saffron." He was still thinking out loud as I listened and tried to not run him off the track of his thought-driven train. I didn't know what to make of this information, but as usual, Coriander seemed to know more than I.

"Why are you so quiet?" He looked at me as if he'd just became aware of my presence.

"I'm not being quiet. I'm giving you time to think," I said.

He looked at me like he wanted to tell me something.

"What is it?"

"Well, it's kind of a long story, but I found this." He pulled out some newspaper clippings and a journal. "This journal belonged to Reed Trustworthy, Hawthorne North Star's butler. He kept careful records."

"Where did you find this?" I asked as I flipped through the journal.

"You know that key you found?"

"Yes."

"I've been doing some snooping of my own, namely in the library. You know that big desk?"

"Yeah."

"This key unlocks that desk." He held it up for me to inspect.

"Wooow," I said slowly.

"At first it appeared empty, but I poked around and this was taped to the top of the desk, inside the drawer. It was as if Reed Trustworthy knew something mysterious was going on before he passed. It's like he wanted to safeguard his carefully acquired information."

I wasn't sure where he was going, so I waited for him to continue.

"I think I should fill you in on what I've learned." He told me the long history of Hawthorne North Star.

"As it is also recorded here, Hawthorne had five children with two wives, four with the first—Hyacinth—and one with the second—unnamed. Mr. Star loved all of his children, but this last one named Saffron had been very difficult for him. The staff called her *detestable* and *horrendous*, but Mr. Star still loved her.

"One day, the staff who had worked for Mr. Star decided they couldn't take her cruelty anymore. They pleaded with him to discipline his unruly daughter. They told him all the bad things she had done to them. When Mr. Star heard all of their complaints, he was troubled, but felt helpless as to what to do. He went to talk to his daughter, but she knew how to manipulate her father. After a short discussion one evening, Saffron was gone the next day. Her room was a mess and her bed was in a pile of disorder. The sight of her room was more than troubling to Hawthorne. He had to sort through the mess to try to figure out what went wrong.

"When Mr. Star understood the evidence of her mess leading to her disappearance, he mourned so deeply that it seemed he would never recover. He never found his beloved daughter, and on his deathbed he asked his butler, Reed Trustworthy, to carry out his wish to open The Hawthorne House for Children—which for some reason is now known as The Children's Horrible House—to help reform unruly children before they could get out of control. He never wanted another parent to feel the pain and shame in losing their child to unruliness. He felt the only way to pay for his lack of discipline for his daughter was to offer a place for rehabilitation to other parents who felt helpless. He also felt an incredible amount of guilt for never having the courage to do the right thing for his daughter. Because even though he loved her very much, he thought that if he were to discipline her, that meant he didn't love her. When he finally understood, it was too late. His guilt and heartbreak compounded until he finally succumbed to his death."

Holly took a seat as she listened, wide-eyed, wondering where the story would go from here.

Coriander continued: "Not long after her father's death, Saffron returned to what she thought was her home. She hadn't been kidnapped, but had faked her disappearance. She thought she could just waltz right on home and get money from her father. But since her father thought she had died, he bequeathed his entire estate to the state. There was no money for her to get. She stormed her way into Reed Trustworthy's office. She tried to throw her fits (which usually got her what she wanted), but this time there was no father to take pity on her. Reed tried to reason with her. She thought he was lying, that there had to be a huge inheritance for her. But when she realized she would get nowhere with all her tantrums, she fled again. Out of desperation for a new beginning, she decided to hop a train. While running to catch the train, she tripped and died. … Ever since her death, The Children's Horrible House has been haunted by her ghost, who still seems to be searching for the hidden treasure."

"That was a lot to take in, Coriander. How do you know all this?" I asked.

"Well, my older sister, Curry, came here not long ago and she found this journal and these newspaper clippings. She put the journal back in the desk where she found it and stashed the key you found under that bed. I looked under every bed myself, but thank heavens you found it and not someone else. When you mentioned the book you found in the library, I thought you were talking about this journal." He walked over to a trunk and laid them out for me to look over. "She would tell me about a lot of this stuff and it became so interesting to me that I had to come here to try to pick up where she left off."

I looked over the clippings. One was the obituary for Hawthorne North Star. Another was an obituary for Saffron Radiant Star. There was also an announcement about the opening of The Hawthorne

House for Children. I looked through the journal that was handwritten in long, angled script. At the top of each page was the date and signature of Reed Trustworthy. This accounting went very far back. He must have been in the employ of Hawthorne North Star for many years.

What he told me about the history of Hawthorne North Star and looking at the newspaper and journal evidence registered in my brain in slow increments. I was still troubled by something. Was it the peacocks or this Saffron's ghost that I heard crying every night? I couldn't forget the ghost we all saw in the white, flowing dress.

"Do you think Saffron's mother is still alive?" I asked. "I wonder what all this has to do with this book." I pointed to the large leather-bound book.

"I think Miss Judge might be able to help us," I told Coriander.

Coriander was reluctant; he didn't seem to trust anyone.

After I thought about it, I felt special because he seemed to trust me. Why else would he have shared this amazing story with me? Then I remembered the PP twins and Clover; did he tell them too? I became suspicious.

I asked him, "Am I the last to know? Did you tell everybody else this already?"

"Not as much as I told you. I told them only what I thought they needed to know in order for them to trust me. I told you *everything* that I have been gathering and putting together. I know there is more and that I am missing a huge piece of the puzzle."

He seemed relieved and dismayed at the same time. Relieved to have someone to talk to, I guessed, but still not sure what to do with all his hard-fought information.

"We're not figuring this out on our own. I say we talk to Miss

Judge; I trust her."

Coriander paid attention to the word *trust* and followed me to the library. On our way there, he wrapped his hand around my arm and stopped me.

"Do you promise me that you will not repeat a word of what I told you to anyone, including Miss Judge?"

I thought about it for a pause and didn't think it would be hard to keep this promise because I would not have been able to repeat it to anyone, even if I wanted. The bits and pieces that were in my brain did fill in the half-drawn picture, but I knew it would be hard for me to actually translate it to anyone. It was like a foreign language that I could hear and understand but could not, for the life of me, speak.

"Yes, I promise."

CHAPTER 37
The North Star Estate

Instead of catching the train or jumping in front of it, Saffron ran back home. She was crushed, but not by the train. She felt that those two options were too easy. She was never lazy. Even if she was malicious and defiant, she never took the easy way out. She waited until morning and asked to see Reed. This time, she had a complete change of posture. She was humble and kind. She was sad and remorseful. She begged Reed to help her.

"I need your help. I've been a horrible person and a horrible daughter. I need to be reformed."

"What do you mean?" Reed asked.

"Could I stay here?" she asked.

"This place is for young children, not for overgrown brats."

"I was a child!" she retorted. "In this house! But no one cared enough to form me right to begin with. ... My mother left me, my father ... well, you know. ... Please help me. I know I have been difficult. I was terrible to everyone, especially my father. At least give me a chance to make up for the pain I caused him and everyone else.

… I'm … sorry."

Reed couldn't believe his ears. Could she honestly be sorry? He thought he would never see the day when Saffron Radiant Star would apologize.

He thought a bit and decided that she was right for once; she should be sorry. And she should pay for all the pain she inflicted on the staff and mostly her father. Reed couldn't think of a better way to make retribution. She was a child who once lived here and was not given the right discipline. He looked at her to see any signs of untruthfulness, but he saw none. She was kneeling at his feet and shaking in fear that he would turn her away. He mercifully agreed to her request.

"Do you promise to go through the whole process without any trouble? I mean the whole process: no special favors, no special treatment, no talking back, no trickery, and no getting away with anything. You will be treated like any other pupil. Do you understand?"

"Yes." She even believed herself at this moment.

"Look at me. Do you promise?"

She looked up. He narrowed his eyes at her to see if he could detect any deceit.

"Yes."

CHAPTER 38
THE CHILDREN'S HORRIBLE HOUSE
THE COSMIC CROSS

When we returned to the library, Miss Judge was not at her desk. We searched for her, but she must have stepped out. I plopped down at the table. Coriander did the same. After a few moments, I wondered what was stopping me from opening the book, and so I went for it. I lifted the heavy, leather-bound cover and my hand softly rubbed the pages. The thick pieces of paper felt like animal skins, only lighter in color and thickness than the leather. I looked at the pictures as well as the writings that were carefully painted. It did not look like a book that had been traditionally printed. Once again, as if the mere opening of the book summoned her, Miss Judge appeared.

Coriander seemed suspicious, but said little. The three of us took turns looking at the pages and examining the meanings. Since all of this was new to me, I didn't have much to add. I was just taking it all in. The two of them bounced ideas around like a tennis match, but I could tell Coriander was being cautious.

Miss Judge explained that the book was very much like the *Farmers' Almanac*. "See here how it includes the names and meanings of the moons? This is how the Native Americans would know the right times to plant and harvest. They used the moon as well as other celestial bodies to guide their gardening before the calendar, as we know it, existed. Funny thing is that with all the technology available to us today, these planting and harvesting tips are still more relevant than any meteorological tools."

My mind was traveling back in time and imagining the native people being so in tune with the Earth as well as its neighboring heavenly bodies, and understanding the relationships among them. I wished I was more in tune with these things. It was like they could understand the language of the entire universe and its messages. Passing these down through generations, they were able to decode many secrets with their acute observations.

As I was thinking, I stared at the title … *Sage Themes*.

Something about the title puzzled me. I said it over and over in my head as the two of them continued to try to correlate the information in the book with current lunar activity. I listened, but it was like my mind was in another place as they were putting pieces together. It was starting to make some sense to me.

The family tree and the image of the empty space where Saffron's mother's name had been etched in my mind formed a nagging entity that began to yell out to me, asking for an explanation: *What about the empty space on the tree? The Star family tree?*

When I blurted out my question to them, the conversation they were engaged in came to a disruptive halt. Miss Judge was the first to attempt to answer my question and as she did, her response gained momentum.

She told us, "Well, in order to answer your question, I need to give you some background information." She paused. "Hawthorne North Star made a small fortune at a young age with the help of his brother, Oleander. He had come from a good family, but he was determined to be successful without the aid of his family. Hawthorne worked for a mercantile company whose owner took Hawthorne under his wing as his protégé. Eventually, Hawthorne and his brother became the owners of the company."

She took a breath, and then continued. "He married Hyacinth as a very wealthy man back in the early twentieth century. He had four children with her, until she passed during childbirth with their last child, Willow. Mr. Star loved all of his children, but the last one, named Saffron, from his new wife, had been very difficult for him. She was what some called *defective*.

"After the passing of his first wife, Hawthorne was sad and alone. He spent a lot of lonely nights staring up into the stars. One of his household staff was a member of the Blackfeet Indian tribe. Her name was Sings-in-the-Meadow and she too was a stargazer. She taught him the ancient art of oneness with the Earth. Their shared interest was a catalyst for their union and they were married. But she was never named or recorded in the family tree because mixing the bloodline was frowned upon by Hawthorne's lineage.

"They had a child, Saffron, and at first lived happily as a family. His wife introduced him to an ancient secret society called One Nation Earth, ONE. It was a secret society of gardeners who used the Native American methods of lunar cycle observations for optimal vegetative growth. They are now called The Garlic Society. They had ancient codes that they followed and they upheld these tenets of this society for generations. Their symbol is the Cosmic Cross, also referred to as the Solar Cross. The cross symbol is encircled, which represents the world, and each bar represents north, south, east and west. The individual elements of air, fire, water, and earth are represented by a circle, and are the four primary forces. These Sacred Four are depicted in the 'Solar' (Cosmic) Cross to maintain balance and their interaction with the sun."

"Like those?" I pointed to the symbols on the library doors. They both looked toward the doors. Coriander looked at Miss Judge as she nodded her head.

"Yes, exactly right," she said. "Did you notice them anywhere else? That symbol can be found throughout the grounds here at The Children's Horrible House. It seems that they are limitless; I find a new one, what must be, daily."

"How many have you found?" Coriander asked.

"Over one hundred," she said. "And they're found in the most obscure places. I even found one in the bathroom."

Miss Judge's face radiated with this tidbit as she continued on with her story. "The society strived for unity with the Earth and all living things and together they were deeply enmeshed. But a huge conflict between Hawthorne's children from his first wife and his Native American wife, Sings-in-the-Meadow, began to tear them apart. Hawthorne felt guilty and torn between them. Sings-in-the-

Meadow began to feel alienated in the white man's world and longed for her own people. One day she was gone. She went back to live with her people, leaving him bereft and with their child, Saffron."

CHAPTER 39
BOARDING SCHOOL

I thought my brain would pop a leak because it felt overstuffed with information. I looked over at Coriander and I could tell that even he had never heard this before. I, for once, was even with him. Forever he had been my guide, ahead of the game, but now we were in the same position.

"So Saffron is the ghost, right?" I wanted to make sure we were on the same page. "She was the daughter of Sings-in-the-Meadow and Hawthorne North Star that everyone hated, right?"

Miss Judge seemed reluctant to agree with this, but instead, offered more. "You see, it's very difficult for a child to lose their mother. Wouldn't you agree?" She looked softly at me.

I thought about the possibility of losing my mother and it made me want to cry.

"Saffron lost her mother at a very young age. And not to a death; hence, she felt abandoned. Having a very sad and confused father made her act out. She was desperate for attention. What every child really craves is a relationship, to feel loved and cared for, like they matter. But everyone was too scared to invest in a relationship with Saffron, most notably her father. He was from a different era, an era where there were boundaries between fathers and children. Children were often not raised by their parents. Many parents hired nannies or caregivers. What he deemed to be the most appropriate way to raise his children was boarding school. He had a hard time forming a relationship with Saffron, but she was the only link to his beloved Sings-in-the-Meadow. ..."

"How do you know all this?" I said, interrupting.

Miss Judge's mouth was on the fast track. However, she quickly diverted her course in order to answer my question. "You don't practically live in a library and not pick up bits and pieces of information, now do you?"

"Sounds like a lot more than bits, if you ask me," Coriander slid in.

"Yeah," I said.

She smiled and reluctantly agreed as well. "The point is that Saffron is not entirely to blame. I know what it's like to not have a parent, you know. Some people handle things differently."

I could tell she felt bad not only for Saffron, but for herself. "I'm sorry, Miss Judge. Did you lose a parent?" I asked.

"Yes, but I don't want to get into that right now." Her face cleared up in an attempt to divert the attention away from her.

I honored her silent request.

CHAPTER 40
Unfinished Business

"Phooey!"

I realized the day was slipping away and the sentences I had to write were not finished. I started to panic. There was no way I'd be able to finish them by the deadline. Why didn't I finish them first, like I'd planned? I was silently scolding myself when Coriander asked me what was wrong.

"I haven't finished writing my sentences and I don't know what will happen to me if I don't!" I went into full panic mode. I went to the table to see how many more sentences I had to complete; I started to count, but knew it wasn't enough.

I sat down and began writing them as fast as I could, when Major Whoopins strode in. I started to shake. What would happen to me? I was so afraid of going to THE DUNGEON. Or what if they put me in that hanging cage I saw when I first came to The Children's Horrible House? My writing became messy as I prayed for instant sentences to magically appear. The sweat from my palms made my pencil drop. I picked it up after wiping my hand on my uniform.

"Young lady," I heard from behind my instantly frozen body. "I'm here to colleck tha' sentences you was required to write as yo' punishment."

I was afraid to look up. So I kept writing, willing my fingers to scribble at supersonic speed.

"Eh-hem," he uttered, clearing his throat.

I could tell his patience was about to be worn out.

Miss Judge spoke on my behalf. "Major Whoopins, it is my fault that Holly was not able to finish her sentences. I asked her to help me with the organization of the books in the library and, well, we lost track of time."

I was deeply grateful for her intervention. Major Whoopins seemed reluctant to allow for this, but he said, "You gon' hafta come wif me."

Oh no, I thought, *I'm really in for it now.* If Miss Judge couldn't talk him out of my punishment, I didn't know who could. I got up and went with him. I looked back at Miss Judge and Coriander, and then at my paper with the unfinished sentences, wishing I could will them to be finished.

We were walking down the hall when Thistle and Nettle snickered and pointed, seeing me in the firm grip of Major Whoopins.

You know how some days seem like they go by so fast and others seem to drag on forever? Well, this was one of those days that had a mix of both. So much had happened in such a short period that I hadn't had any time to eat dinner. But because I had been so busy, I hadn't noticed my hunger until now. Lucky for me, Major Whoopins was leading me into the dining hall.

Along the way, I saw the twins eating dinner without me. When we came to the food line, we walked past it and into the kitchen.

A stack of dishes was piled up to the ceiling, each dish covered in crusty old food.

Major Whoopins placed me in front of the sink, grabbed an apron and a step stool for me, and said, "Do these here dishes and do them right, and maybe I'll git you some extra time fo' those sentences."

CHAPTER 41
DREAMS AND NIGHTMARES, THERE'S A DIFFERENCE

The tower of dishes kept growing as I kept washing, but eventually they stopped coming and I made some progress.

The loudspeaker blared into the kitchen: "Mr. Mungus, we have a code puke; a code puke in the dining hall."

A balding man wearing a dirty white tank top, drooping white pants, and an even dirtier white apron obediently reached for the mop bucket and some bleach before heading out to do his dirty job.

"Thanks, Hugh," Miss Shapen said as Mr. Mungus sloshed his way toward the mess.

I was glad *I* didn't have to clean up someone's barf.

Miss Shapen liquidly walked over to inspect my work. She wiped her index finger across a few dishes, making sure no grease was left behind. "Not baaaaad," she bleated, like a goat.

I was exhausted from what seemed to be my eternal day.

After getting the okay from Miss Shapen, the lunch lady, Major

Whoopins took me to my room. We walked silently. I had nothing to offer in conversation and he didn't seem to care. I stepped into my room and dropped into bed in the clothes I had been wearing all day. I felt dirty, but too exhausted to change.

Unfortunately, my uncleanliness, or the loud thunderstorm that moved in as I was sleeping, kept me in a state of restlessness even though at moments I must have drifted to sleep. It was a long night of tossing and turning, wishing I had bathed or finished my sentences or didn't have to wash dishes. The lightning flashes were striking all around the house like a strobe blinking in brief, repetitive spells. I kept feeling anxiety over not finishing my sentences. It was this circular track that kept whirling around in my head like a washing machine. The dishes kept coming and they were filled with food that I wanted to eat, but when I nearly put the food in my mouth, it was rotten meatloaf; then it transformed into a cow's tongue that tried to lick my face as I tried to eat it, leaving me with a cowlick in my hairline that stuck up on the right side of my head. It tickled as the tongue licked my cheek and forehead, and my face was glazed in cow slobber. Then I saw the face of my cow back home, Roger. He was a big Black Angus cow who had eyes as large as crabapples. He mooed.

I didn't want to eat Roger!

I heard the mooing again.

I woke up drenched in dirty sweat.

"*MOOOOOVE! MOOOVE!*" I heard one of the girls urging.

I couldn't see clearly and was confused, so I got up and used the bathroom, washed my face, brushed my teeth, and gave myself a thorough sponge bath. I changed into my clean bedclothes and slipped back into bed. I felt so much better. The lightning had lessened and the rain's white noise aided my return to slumber.

In deep sleep later that night, I dreamed of the vegetable garden. I was at one end, surrounded by tall husks of corn. The moon was high and full; I couldn't see a path through the garden. Then I was in the maze garden and I kept getting stuck at each turn, with nowhere to pass. I heard a howl that seemed close. My hairs stood up like a scaredy-cat's fur. Then I heard a growl. I turned and saw a wolf bent down, with saliva dripping from his gnarled, rumbling sneer. *It's okay,* I told myself. ... *He can't hurt me,* I affirmed.

My subconscious was trying to tell me that I was sleeping and this was only a dream, but another consciousness kept creeping in and making my bad dream feel like reality. I tried to let the positive voice win, but my affirmations vanished when the wolf charged me.

I wanted to escape, but was afraid to turn my back to the wolf. When I turned around I saw Clover's face; she was horrified at the approaching animal. When I took off, the maze had disappeared, along with Clover. I was running in the open field, with nowhere to hide. My running became hindered by the heavy book I was holding. I could not go fast. My legs sank into the ground as I continued, but it became like I was running in quicksand. My body clenched into a tight ball as I tried to protect it from certain attack. When I turned to see the wolf attack me, Coriander stood there wondering why I was so scared.

"What are you doing? You're all rolled up like a roly-poly." He laughed.

"Don't you see that wolf? It's going to bite me and shred me to tiny pieces." I explained the wolf to Coriander, but it was like I was trying to convince him of something that didn't exist. Ignoring my fears, he helped me up. At first I staggered, lining up my feet with difficulty.

Our walk steadied as we glided together in the garden toward the mausoleum. The glowing garden was on fire and spreading. It was as if the fireflies turned into patches of flames throughout. I looked for all the familiar trees and flowers, but the garden was almost unrecognizable except for the unmistakable dome on top of the building. I could see flames from within. It was on fire too. I turned to leave when it started raining heavily.

"I'm getting out of here! I'm scared, Coriander!"

But Coriander stood in front of me and blocked my exit by holding up the book that had once been in my arms. Through my blurred vision, I could see him mouthing something, but couldn't hear him. I cupped my ears and focused on his face as he repeated, "I have a message."

"What is it?" I asked, but my voice sounded like it was underwater.

Then, as if he spoke from a megaphone, he said, *"I HAVE THE MESSAGE."*

I jolted up out of my dream, sweating and breathing heavily. It seemed important in my dream, like it was another one of those nagging thoughts knocking around in my head, begging to be taken seriously.

Even though I awoke, I was still in twilight and fell quickly back to sleep. The dreams continued as I slept.

Every time I completed a page of sentences that Director Pankins had me write, the sentences disappeared. I rewrote them over and over but they would be gone. It was like I wrote them in vanishing pencil lead. I became so worried, I got up and paced back and forth across the darkly lit library. I picked up the pace and was running, but this time nothing was chasing me. I realized I was running *to* something—to catch a train. The car doors were open and waiting for me, but I was too scared to make the leap. The speed of the train kept changing as I finally summoned the courage to make the leap. I was afraid I wouldn't make it and then be crushed by the train, but I kept running and running, then I ran faster than the train and I beat it like we were in a race.

I ran to tell my parents about my superfast running, but when I got home, I was standing in front of The Children's Horrible House and my parents were nowhere to be found.

CHAPTER 42
SUCH RELIEF

When I woke the next morning the dreams seemed faint, yet I still remembered them clearly enough. I didn't want to remember the last one because it made me feel sad. So I put that one in the "Don't Remember" file of my brain. I could remember the one I had before that, and I couldn't wait to see Coriander. I wanted to tell him my dream.

When I found him, it was like we both were excited to see each other, to tell one another something extra important. We started to speak at the same time.

"No, you go first. No, you go first," we both said.

I went first and told him all about my dream.

His face lit up like an arcade game. "You are never going to believe this," he said. "My dream was very similar, but it was more detailed. I think I figured a lot out … the book, the dates, the plants, and the treasure. But we won't know for sure unless we are in the right place on the full moon. My guess is that something spectacular will take place near or inside the mausoleum."

"Wow," I said, astounded.

"How did you ever put all that together? Just from your dream?"

"Well, yes and no; actually it wasn't that easy. I took your advice and talked more with Miss Judge. She really knows a lot about this place and even more about Hawthorne North Star. And you were right; I think we can trust her. Miss Spelling's class, as well as the others, has been filling in a lot of holes too, plus I've been doing a lot of observations and paying attention to the little things about this place. I found that if you pay attention to the little things, you can figure out the big things." His explanation was punctuated with enthusiasm.

"That wasn't the only dream I had last night," I ruefully told him. I described the anxiety. "I still feel like I need to complete writing those sentences, or they are going to haunt my dreams forever. I still don't understand why I'm not in THE DUNGEON right now. I was sure I'd be getting a much worse punishment from Director Pankins. I wonder what happened."

After a small pause, Coriander explained to me why I wasn't in THE DUNGEON. "After you left with Major Whoopins, I finished writing the sentences. I hoped that was okay with you. I didn't want you to get in any more trouble."

I was at a loss. The relief I felt was compounded with gratefulness. Those feelings fled, replaced with panic. "What if they can tell the difference in our handwriting? What if you get in trouble too?"

"Don't worry. I'm an expert when it comes to copying handwriting. That's one of the reasons I'm here. I wrote myself too many excuses for absences in school. I mastered my mother's signature to a *T*. Plus, when Major Whoopins came back to get the sentences, he never said a thing about it to me. And if I was going to be in trouble, it would have happened already, right? I would be in **THE DUNGEON**, right?"

I did feel better, but not one hundred percent. I decided to push those thoughts to the side and concentrate on our mission. We had to find the hidden treasure of Hawthorne North Star.

CHAPTER 43
BACK TO THE GRIND

The beds I made were a work of art. I really found a lot of pleasure in making them now. When I cleaned the rooms, I imagined the grandness of the architecture and the beautiful furnishings. I made sure the furnishings were in the perfect place and I dusted all the knickknacks. I never would have imagined that I'd enjoy cleaning, but it gave me time to think.

Later, at lunch, I joined Staniel and Danley. Clover wasn't there yet. I sat and started to eat. They got up at the same time and sat at the next table, pretending to ignore me.

"Guys. Is there something wrong? Are you mad at me?"

They glanced at me and looked away.

I asked myself, *What did I do?* I searched and racked my brain. I said to them, "Did I do something?"

Staniel seemed to melt a bit, but was still snarky. "Where's your boyfriend? Why don't you sit with him?"

"My boyfriend? Yuck. I don't have a boyfriend! What are you talking about?"

"Coriander," they accusingly said.

"Coriander is not my boyfriend. He is just my friend … who happens to be a boy. But no, he is not my boyfriend. Like you guys. You are my friends too, right?"

"We thought so," Danley said, "but you told us to leave you alone and it seems like you only have time for us when he's not around. Even Clover says so."

"Clover? Where is Clover?" I asked while giving the cafeteria a quick scan.

They pointed across the room. She was sitting with *THEM*. I almost could not believe my eyes. What was she doing? They were all laughing too. I could see straight down big bucktoothed Thistle's mouth. I swear a dragon lived in there. I was sure it smelled like a dumpster or toe jam. I wanted to get up and claim my friend, but I was too intimidated by two things—okay, three. Thistle and Nettle, as well as **THE DUNGEON** … okay, four … that hanging cage thing too.

It wasn't just them sitting there; Cherry was too. She was gloating over the reestablished friendship with Clover. Then all four looked over at me, made goofy expressions, and laughed. I turned red. My hurt and anger boiled inside. They were taking my friend and turning her against me. They had bullied me and done everything they could to make my life irksome, but this was the final straw.

The food I had wanted to eat very badly now seemed inedible.

The four of them got up at the same time and left D-Hall together. Clover didn't even look over at me. Staniel and Danley came back to my table with no words to offer, but a silent apology. This gentle act of mercy cooled my emotions and I was grateful to them. It also gradually reinstated my appetite. I ate everything on my tray and the three of us left together.

As we were walking back to our classes, I told them about the dreams that Coriander and I had had, and how we were going to find the treasure. They were back on board. It doesn't feel good to be left out, and I knew this feeling all too well. I wanted to make sure my friends didn't feel that way. I wished I could have made Clover understand this; I hoped it wasn't too late. I hoped they didn't turn her totally against me.

In the days that passed, I felt Clover's friendship move further and further away. I thought about it as I made the beds and cleaned the rooms. The three—Thistle, Nettle, and Cherry—never missed a moment to sneer in my direction or laugh, hoping to communicate to me that I was on the outside of their foursome. Clover wouldn't make eye contact.

One day as I was making a bed, Thistle and Nettle ran in and deliberately messed it up. I ignored them and fixed it as soon as they left. I hated the feeling of being powerless, but didn't know what else to do. Another day as I was using the bathroom, they held the door closed so I couldn't get out. They were laughing hysterically. I wondered how they were able to get away with all these antics without getting caught. Then one day, in the dining hall, something clicked. I was eating my food with Staniel. Danley was on his way with his tray.

The four girls, including Cherry and Clover, were walking our way, when Thistle and Nettle walked up to our table and pushed my tray away from my seat. Thistle said, "This is *our* table."

I didn't give myself any time to think. I stood with my fists balled up, and put my face right in theirs and said as firmly and as loudly as possible, "Who is gonna make me move?" I realized that I was actually eye to eye with them and for some reason I must have magically grown, because I felt huge and unstoppably brave.

The whole cafeteria was silent as the two backed off and pretended to be cool as they halfheartedly snickered. They knew as well as everyone else who won this spat, and it wasn't them. I turned halfway around and saw that Staniel and Danley were firmly placed at my right and left. They surrounded me, making me appear bigger and more threatening. It was good to know that my true friends were there to back me up when I needed them.

"Come on, Clover." Cherry pulled at her arm, but Clover jerked it away from her.

Clover said, "I think I'll stay here with my friends, thank you."

"I thought I was your friend," Cherry stated.

"Yeah, us too," the thorny girls said.

"I don't need friends like you." She put her arms around Staniel and Danley, who both put their hands on my shoulders, and Clover proudly said, "I need good friends like these two and Holly."

Cherry snubbed up her nose and said, "Whatever, losers."

"Yeah, whatever. You detherve each other," bucktooth said.

"Well, you deserve a breath mint, 'cause your breath smells like you ate a dumpster filled with horse farts!" I retorted.

Silence. … Then the whole cafeteria roared in laughter with hoots and hollers. This was one of the many putdowns Ginger had inflicted on me, which I was now grateful to her for its timely use. The three girls flicked their hair as they turned and walked away.

At this point all of the blood and courage that boosted me to stand up and defend myself deflated as I imagined what could have happened.

"I'm sorry, Holly," Clover said as if she were a mouse.

I nodded and accepted her apology, no questions asked. The rest of the kids in the cafeteria came up to me in groups and congratulated me on my performance. A lot of them I didn't even know, but now I felt part of a huge circle of friends. They made me feel included and special. A couple of other kids told me that seeing me stand up to those bullies gave them the courage to stand up for themselves too.

CHAPTER 44
RESTORATION

We were all back together. It's funny how fragile and how strong friendships can be. Some are easy, some have to be nurtured, and some are difficult. But the bottom line is, it's always better when we're all together. Of course the boys still had fun with their little jabs, but it was nice that even though we had our differences, we were united.

The five of us worked together and came up with a plan. We put all of our individually gained pieces together.

The date arrived.

To say that the excitement in the air was palpable was a huge understatement. But I could be exaggerating. ... My mother often said, "Holly, I've told you a billion times to stop exaggerating!" But I was pretty sure she had not *told me* a *billion times*, maybe twenty or thirty times at the most.

I went to work making the beds and cleaning the rooms with so much enthusiasm. It was like I had extra energy, knowing that tonight was the night. I think the smile I woke up with became permanently placed on my face.

As I was admiring one of my freshly made beds, Major Whoopins came into the room and said, "Come wit' me, please." He sounded serious.

The rest of the kids became silent as I went with him.

I followed him to Director Pankins' office. He opened the door and signaled for me to enter. Director Pankins was seated at her desk, but with her back to me. I could see her looking up at the portrait above her head. It was elegant how the woman and child were artistically captured. I sat in the empty chair and waited for her to turn around. After a long pause, her chair slowly swiveled to face me.

"I understand you did not complete the sentences you were instructed to write," she calmly stated.

Oh, no. I thought Coriander had taken care of that. I was afraid those unfinished sentences would come back to haunt me. I slumped my shoulders and looked down. There was no use in denial.

"It's true. I didn't finish them."

"Who did?"

I looked over to Major Whoopins, who shifted his gaze out the window and began to whistle.

"Not I," I truthfully told her.

She said slowly, "Tell me who."

I didn't want Coriander to get in trouble too, so I decided to keep my mouth shut.

"I don't know." I figured that since I never saw him write them, I really didn't know who did. But he told me he did, so I did know— but that was not important right now.

"Since you *don't know* ... or can't conveniently remember, maybe spending time in THE DUNGEON will jog your memory."

"Isn't the Star Day celebration this evening?" she asked Major Whoopins. "It's a shame you'll be missing out."

Director Pankins was toying with me like I had seen my cat do with doomed birds and lizards.

It was a shame. I had been looking forward to this celebration since the day Miss Gyde told us about it.

"If you tell me who finished these for you, we may be able to work something out." She held up the papers for me to examine, enticing me to tell on my friend. My mouth refused to be a tattletale and I remained quiet. I looked directly at her and pretended to zip my lips.

"Take her to **THE DUNGEON**," she commanded Major Whoopins.

* * *

"Why didn't you just tell her?" Major Whoopins asked as we made our way through the hallways and down to **THE DUNGEON**.

"Why did *YOU* tell her?" I accused him.

"Oh, no! You don't take that tone wit' me, young lady." He unlocked the huge door and signaled for me to enter. "You go on 'head and git inside. Shoulda wrote yo' sentences in tha' firs' place!" He shook his head in disappointment. Then I saw the look of regret at having to close the door in my face.

"I'm sorry, Holly. I … I really am." He looked down and shut the door.

CHAPTER 45
The North Star Estate

From the third-floor room that she claimed as her own, Saffron looked through the lens of the unusually high-definition telescope her father used to study the universe. His wealth and vast intelligence provided technology much more advanced than the average stargazing citizen.

She admired her new role as she walked around her vantage-positioned room. *That wasn't so hard,* she thought. *I did it all.* The beds were made, the rooms cleaned, the dishes done. She even learned more about the three subjects she was secretly interested in; astronomy, horticulture, and meteorology were the same subjects her mother and father obsessed over. Plus, she found her own interest in them during her training. She knew they would be useful in her quest. She graduated with flying colors. Upon Saffron's graduation, she decided that the spoiled, bratty girl she once was died the night she ran for the train. She even had a funeral held for Saffron Radiant Star; *she* was dead.

She renamed herself Sirius Pankins (after the huge radiating star and for the punishments that spoiled children deserve). She couldn't wait to dole out the spankings on these children that infested her house. After the untimely death of Reed Trustworthy, she became director of *this* Children's Horrible House, which she appropriately renamed as well. Sirius Pankins made sure that the remaining staff members of The Hawthorne House for Children were fired. A new staff who were not privy to her past were hired. She was confident that her inheritance was in this giant enigmatic home somewhere. During her chores, she spotted some clues, but her father was a very wise man.

"I will find it one day, I'm sure I will, even if I have to use these horrible children to find it for me," she promised herself as she looked deep into the cloud-filled background of the portrait of herself and her mother.

CHAPTER 46
THE CHILDREN'S HORRIBLE HOUSE
CRIME AND PUNISHMENT

I felt defeated, like all the energy I had earlier had sprung a leak and seeped out until it was empty. I imagined the big celebration that I was now missing. I figured the Star Day celebrations were already under way. It would be a huge celebration this year because it was the twenty-fifth anniversary. It was a day of games and festivities. I imagined there would be tug-o'-war, relay races, potato sack races, and an egg toss. My favorite was the dunk tank. In my head, we were taking turns dunking Mr. Mungus, mean old Mr. Meanor, and even Major Whoopins!

There would have to be hot dogs and hamburgers, baked beans, potato salad, my favorite deviled eggs, and cotton candy. My mouth watered … I could taste the delectable party foods expediently in my imagination.

Then I heard some booms. They sounded like fireworks! I loved fireworks! And I was missing out on them while everyone else was having a blast. I got up and started to pace around the room, when I remembered the secret room that I saw Director Pankins come out of before.

"Where is it?" I was almost startled by my own echoing voice. I was touching the walls, looking for an access. Nothing seemed apparent to open the secret door. I looked on the floor and noticed that my shoe was untied. As I bent down to tie it, my butt hit something like a lever and then the hidden door opened with what looked like a demon bird flying into my face, ready to peck out my eyeballs! I slammed my eyes shut and screamed loud as a banshee!

"Cuckoo! Cuckoo!" I heard as I timidly opened my eyes. The rush of adrenaline left me stiffened as I realized that it wasn't some beastly bird attacking me. It was a cuckoo clock announcing the top of the hour.

"Blasted bird," I scolded as I recomposed myself. What was a dumb old cuckoo clock doing all the way down here? I thought as I was flooded with the fresh scent of horse manure. I gagged and covered my nose and mouth with my left sleeve.

I noticed a toilet paper roll ... probably the same one that lost a couple of sheets to the bottom of Director Pankins' high-heeled shoe. I wondered what that was doing in here. A sliver of light coming from the bottom of the far wall caught my eye. I saw that there was a door, but it must have only opened from the outside. I got down on my hands and knees to see if there was anything on the other side. I saw grass and leaves. It looked like it was the outside. The floor I stood on was roughly leveled dirt, so I grabbed the shovel they used to garden and started to dig. The dirt was thick and heavy.

I dug for what seemed like hours, but it couldn't have been that long, I thought, as I wiped my brow. I was making progress, and lauded myself.

I excavated a little tunnel big enough for my body to shimmy through. As I was crawling like a soldier trying to not trigger any explosives, earthworms wriggled around, blindly looking for soil to enrich. I felt something slither over my legs. What was that? I closed up my body like a clam and scrambled outside faster than a jackrabbit.

I stood and dusted off all the dark dirt and began to run, until I ran into a large cart. On the side, I could barely make out the words: *MANURE SPREADER*. Yuck. I jumped back, but knew I had to hurry so I quickly ran around it. I was steps from the maze garden, but right now I had to find my friends.

I made it just in time to see the celebration being capped off with a brilliant display of floating lanterns released into the night sky. They were in all different shapes and colors. For a minute I wasn't sure if I was breathless from all the digging or at the magnificent sight. I loved the beautiful radiance showing as they gently floated up toward the heavens. I was enjoying the dazzling display as I noticed the giant moon begin its ascent. It seemed unusually large and orangey red.

I needed to find everyone, but I couldn't be caught. I ran to some bushes and tried to spot my friends.

"Where are they?" I asked myself, and impatiently looked around. Then I saw Clover and the PP twins looking up.

I ran over and said, "Where were you?"

"We were looking for you, silly! Where were you?"

"Oh." I just remembered they didn't know where I had been. "I was in THE DUNGEON."

"What? Did you get a *spankin'*?" Staniel playfully asked.

"No! But I thought I was going to miss out on Star Day and everything else. I almost wished I would have gotten a *spankin'* and then it would have been over with," I informed him.

"I hate to break up this pity party, but we need to go get Coriander," Danley warned.

"What? Where is he?" I said, panic in my voice.

"He's in the hanging cage. We tried to get him out, but nothing worked," Clover said.

Without waiting to hear more, I ran around the giant building and came to the front. There he was, slouching inside the cage, all alone. How was I going to help?

"Coriander, it's me, Holly."

"Hey, Holly," he said sadly.

"I'll get you out of there!"

"How?"

I didn't have the answer, but knew I'd think of something. I looked around to see if there was anything I could throw up to him, but everything seemed too big or not helpful. Clover and the twins showed up, breathless.

"What's the plan?" Staniel asked.

"What's keeping you from getting out?" I asked Coriander.

"This lock." He shook the cage door.

I looked around trying to find something that could pick the lock—when I remembered my hairpin. I reached into my pocket and found the hairpin I had used to unlock the attic door. I was grateful for the super-deep buttoned pockets in my coveralls. It was worth a shot … but how would I get it up to him?

I grabbed a long light stick. "Does anyone have some string?" I asked.

"I have this ribbon," Clover replied.

I took it and tied the hairpin to the stick.

"You ready? I'm going to throw this stick up to you and you can use the hairpin to unlock the door."

I tossed it. It floated up and landed perfectly in his waiting hands.

"Good plan," everyone said, hoping.

Coriander unwrapped the string and freed the hairpin.

"Here goes nothin'," he said as he wiggled the pin around in the lock. He wiggled and wiggled, nothing happened. Then, out of frustration he wiggled extra hard and "POP," the cage door opened.

We cheered! But realized that he was too high to jump down. I ran to the woods and grabbed a pile of leaves. Everyone else followed and grabbed more, stacking a soft pile for Coriander to land on without breaking any bones.

He carefully climbed out and hung from the bottom of the cage.

"Jump!" the twins called to him.

He seemed scared, but then he closed his eyes and let go. The three of us, along with the pile of twigs and leaves, cushioned his fall.

"Thanks, you guys!"

Coriander laid on us for a long couple of seconds until we all pushed him off.

"You helped us out plenty. It's the least we could do for you," Danley stated.

"Yeah," Staniel said.

"Enough with all this mushy stuff," Coriander said. If we don't put our plan into action, we might miss our chance."

"Oh, yeah! It's about to happen!" Danley rubbed his hands together in excitement.

We all looked at each other like we were kids waiting for Santa to come on the night before Christmas. In a few short hours the moon would be in the right position for the treasure to be unlocked.

CHAPTER 47
COSMIC SHOW

There was a lot of buzz around that evening as the children were corralled back into the house. It was a perfect night to be unnoticed. As far as Director Pankins knew, I was in THE DUNGEON and Coriander was in the hanging cage.

We hid in the thicket of trees just beyond the open field where the festivities were held. We were discussing our plan when the time came for us to make our move. One by one, we entered the maze garden. We skipped our way through the labyrinthine maze and jumped in elation as we came to the elegant entrance within. The bright full moon provided all the light we needed. It also made it easy for someone to see us if they were looking for us. We had to be careful. We had to be stealthy in order to carry out our mission.

As we came into the glowing garden, I realized I could spend the rest of my life here and never be bored at the sight. It was sensational and spine-tingling. The lightning bugs blinked, signaling us to enter. It was nice to see that they weren't on fire, like in my bad dream. The weeping willow tree welcomed us with its humble posture. I bowed back, just like Mr. Ree. The floating orbs greeted us and followed us as the scent of the night-blooming jasmine lured us to the entrance of the tomb. I could smell it when we stepped under the arbor filled with brilliant blooming passionflowers. I was sure my mother would love these. I picked one and put it in my pocket.

I saw the group of white peacocks high in the trees. Their heads were tucked in for the night and they weren't moving. That was a good sign.

We stood outside the door and wondered how to get in. We nosed around and poked at the different holes in the wall, and pulled on what could have been levers, but found nothing. Then Coriander discovered five circles that looked like place holders in the cement of the threshold. They had crosses inside them like the ones for The Garlic Society—Hawthorne North Star's secret society—and they formed a star.

A light illuminated in Coriander's brain as he directed us to step into the shallow indentations. As we did so, the door to the mausoleum descended into the ground, allowing us to enter what looked like a sheathed sacred place. We stepped behind the thick velvet curtain, into an interior room where torches were magically lit. They were casting a glow that allowed for limited but sufficient sight. In the center of the room lay a concrete casket, directly under the dome of what appeared to be a planetarium. Glass holes were cut into the dome in the shape of different constellations. I recognized them, but didn't remember all the names.

"Hey, check this out," Staniel said.

Danley pointed. "Look down; look at those. Don't they look like the same things that we stepped on in order to open the tomb?"

Coriander, Clover, and I looked at where they pointed. The

same circular cross place holders lay on the ground, surrounding the casket. If you could draw an imaginary line connecting them all, it would form another star and the casket was in the center. We walked around and instinctively took our places. The five of us formed a perfect star which surrounded Hawthorne North Star's final resting place.

The moon was making its way up into the sky. As it got higher, it glowed brighter and smaller.

Coriander excitedly said, "It's coming. It's about to happen, you guys. Be ready."

We waited anxiously. It seemed that time stood still. I closed my eyes to see if the moon was moving. I counted up to thirty Mississippi. When I opened my eyes, I could totally see the changes. The moon was clearly making its way to its position.

"When the moon comes into place, we will only have a few moments before it moves again and we might lose our chance to get the treasure." Coriander was very nervous that it would pass us by and we would have done all this work and research for nothing. "It's almost like a stellar puzzle that will come together automatically," he added.

Then, as if it were scheduled for an important meeting, the moon slid into the dead center of the dome, lighting the inside like a spotlight; but not only the moon … so did the constellations. The ceiling lit up in a fantastic cosmic exhibition, where we were not only spectators, but also participants. I could clearly make out the North Star located at the base of Ursa Minor. Leo, the lion, lit up the dome like a king ruling his celestial pride. Then the crowning star we had all been waiting to see, showed up and stole the show.

The Star of Panivita penetrated the planetarium like a divine revelation. Sounds of music from the universal spheres echoed in the dome like heralding angels. The rays of light it reflected bounced from wall to wall like a laser show. The light danced and sparkled throughout the room and when it came close to my eyes, it was blinding. I closed them and could still see the movements of the light show from behind my eyelids; it was that bright. When I opened my eyes, all I could see was what looked like glitter vision or the static on the television screen. Slowly, the light steadied and my normal vision was restored.

Like a key with the right compositions, the casket opened with a mist-filled cloud thicker than fog. The air became unbreathable. We were all choking and coughing, but when it finally dissipated, we were surprised to see no body in the casket. We were expecting and dreading the thought of what was in the box, but I, for one, was half-relieved and disappointed that it was empty. Where was Hawthorne North Star? Did his body disappear? Was it ever buried here? Or did it already decompose to nothingness?

Coriander wafted away the stubborn mist that clung to the sides of the casket. The only thing he found was a book that looked to be buried or placed within the center of the casket. So that if a body were inside the casket, it would be covering the book. A coat of dust rested on the top cover.

Coriander blew on the book, making the dust scatter into a cloud.

"Hey," Clover said, coughing, "watch where you blow that!"

Coriander was too excited to be careful, but he did say, "Sorry, Clover."

Everyone gathered around the book. Staniel and Danley read the title together: "*The Message.*"

I looked over to Coriander, who was already looking at me. It appeared similar to the book we had found in the library, but this one was slightly different.

"Is it the same as the book in the library?" I asked.

"It must be related to it because if you look at the two titles, they have all the same letters but they are arranged differently," Staniel stated.

"It's an anagram," Danley casually said.

"An anawhat?" Coriander asked.

"Hey, I thought you knew everything," Danley joked.

"My secret is out; I don't know everything," Coriander confessed.

Staniel informed us, "An anagram is a type of word game. It's where you take a word and rearrange the letters to make a new word. See, this book is called *The Message*, and if you take all these letters and put them in a different order, they spell *Sage Themes*."

That was undeniably really cool. "But what's the point?" I asked.

They both shrugged. "Sorry, that's all we got," said the twins.

Clover hadn't said a whole lot up to this point. Maybe she still felt bad about her temporary friendship with Nettle and Thistle.

"Maybe one gives words of wisdom and the other one gives words to live by. 'Sage' is an herb, and it also means wisdom. 'Themes' are a person's thoughts or writings. Maybe it's, kind of like, *Words of Wisdom*."

Coriander opened up *The Message*.

It appeared to be a collection of books told from many different points of view. Inside was the history and lineage of the Star family. It had many stories of Hawthorne's long-lost ancestors. It would take too long to actually read every word of this book, and we didn't have that kind of time, but as we flipped through, we noticed one page that was folded in half in the dead center of the book. And in the center of the page, one line was written in bold letters, it read:

> "For where your treasure is,
> your heart will be also."

"What the heck?" I said, disappointed.

"Yeah. What is that supposed to mean?" Coriander asked.

Was this book the treasure? How was this old book the treasure? Was there even a treasure at all? Or were we all part of a huge prank?

While we were flipping through, looking for any clues as to how to proceed, Director Pankins came in like a bolt of lightning and said, "I'll take that!" She took it and motioned for her crew to shoo us out.

"Actually, I'll take that!" Miss Judge popped up in her usual book-summoning fashion, but this time she was dressed in a long, white, flowing gown, just like the one we saw the first time we saw the ghost. She grabbed the book from Director Pankins, rendering her stunned and silent for an instant. We were all stunned and still as standing stones, waiting for some spell to be broken.

Director Pankins looked her up and down, visibly miffed at this intrusion and impertinence. "Just who do you think you are, Mrs. What's Your Name?"

"I am the rightful heir to this book, this estate, and to the hidden treasure," Miss Judge courageously informed her.

Major Whoopins and Mr. Ree were not sure if they should intervene. And it seemed Director Pankins' curiosity compelled her to verify the truthfulness to her claim.

"That is not possible," Director Pankins stated, "because the rightful heir you speak of would be me."

The five of us were shocked by this impasse. How was this possible? There were no known heirs to Hawthorne's fortune. That is why he left it to the state, as the story goes.

"I am Willow Faint Star, the last child Hawthorne Star had with his wife, Hyacinth. I was raised by my grandparents until they passed. So I returned home ... my rightful home." Miss Judge drove in her last point with serious conviction.

We gasped in the learning of this revelation. It seemed that Director Pankins was definitely not prepared for this battle and she seemed reluctant to say a word about this claim. But instead of going mute, she threw out a major truth bomb.

"Hmmm ... I guess we're sisters," she said casually and as if she was okay with this news.

"What do you mean?" It was Miss Judge's turn to be bamboozled.

"My name is Saffron Radiant Star, daughter of Hawthorne North Star and *his wife*, Sings-in-the-Meadow." She laid out her case as if there were no need for cross-examination.

"I thought you were dead," I inadvertently said. I shouldn't have said those words, but those words successfully snuck out when others hadn't.

As if they just became aware of the meddling brats who invaded their family reunion, they both signaled Major Whoopins and Mr. Ree to take us out.

"No! Don't make us leave! *NOOOOOOOO!*"

But our protests were ignored. The only ones affected by our cries were the peacocks who were prancing around, now calling for what sounded like, *"HAAALP! HAAALP!"*

Mean old Mr. Meanor and the rest of the waiting troops picked us up and toted us around like luggage being loaded onto an airplane.

We were carried out, but not only out of the garden and into the field. We were being taken away from The Children's Horrible House. I know this will sound weird, but I didn't want to leave. We worked too hard to have our treasure swooped out from under us. Well, we didn't exactly find the treasure, but we were close, so close! I could just feel it! Now we'd never find out, and I bet either Miss Judge or Director Pankins was in the process of stealing our rightful treasure.

CHAPTER 48
THE TREASURE

Where were we going? Mr. Ree was driving again, and Major Whoopins was there to oversee our transportation. It was like when Coriander and I were driven *to* The Children's Horrible House. The others—Clover, Staniel, and Danley—were taken in another van to who knows where. We traveled silently at first, our thoughts too loud for any real conversations to occur. I turned to look at Coriander. His expression told me everything; he was *MAD*. I didn't blame him; I was mad too.

"I guess it wasn't meant to be," I said, trying to comfort him.

"Humph," was his only reply as he crossed his arms in an attempt to keep from exploding.

We drove for hours throughout the night. Like a lamp in the darkness, the full moon followed, lighting our path. Its soft glow lulled me to sleep. The trance that I fell into was so deep and restful, I felt like I was unconscious. I heard nothing and felt nothing for an unknown amount of time.

I slowly became foggily aware of some sounds. They were flickering around in my head like a hummingbird. What were they?

A faint tune. Someone was singing. I could make out a melody of some sort. It was fading in and out. I saw a figment of a woman floating on a cloud in outer space. She was surrounded by stars, the moon, and planets, which seemed to make music as she reached out her hand in their direction. It was like she was a conductor in a star symphony. She was singing along with the cosmic tune as she made her way down to Earth. The cloud she was riding on disappeared in a poof upon her landing.

She was wearing animal skins, black moccasins, and lots of brightly colored stones as jewelry. She had dark, flowing hair and a beautiful smiling face. She landed in a patch of abundant wildflowers that her hands brushed as she glided through the meadow. She was singing in a foreign language as she walked toward a man I hadn't noticed before. He was tall, with hair so light it looked like the cloud she was just riding. He looked older than her, but there was a noticeable attraction between them. She greeted him with a kiss and said, "Hello, my love."

He followed saying, "Hello, my heart ..."

I woke with a feeling that I was falling. I jerked and gasped out the words, "Sings-in-the-Meadow!"

That's where the treasure was! It was with his heart! I quoted the verse I saw in the book: "For where your treasure is, your heart will be also."

"What are you babbling about, Butt Sphincter?" My sister Ginger's voice appeared out of my subconsciousness.

"Huh? Where am I?"

"Duh, in your room ... like always," she snipped as she passed through the hallway wrapped in a towel, with curlers dangling from her hair.

I blinked and sat up. I was in my room. … Wait a second. I WAS IN MY ROOM! How did I get back here without waking up? Was it all a dream? It seemed so real, too real to be a dream. I looked at my clothes: no more white coveralls. I was wearing the clothes I wore to The Children's Horrible House, but they didn't look or smell dirty. I sniffed. My hands sprung to my head and felt the bunny-eared hat snuggling my short-haired head.

"I'm coming up to inspect," my mother's singsongy voice sang.

"Oh, no! I'm going to be in trouble." My hands came up and covered my eyes and glasses, hoping that if I couldn't see, then maybe no one could see me. I hadn't cleaned my room. I must have fallen asleep before I started cleaning.

But when my mother came to my door, she smiled. "Guess you're not going to The Children's Horrible House after all."

"Huh?" I was squinting, sure I would be in heaps of trouble. When I opened my eyes I realized that I wasn't lying on the pile of clothes and laundry I'd flung my body on top of before.

I sat up and clambered to my knees and looked at my bed. My bed was made beautifully. I had never made my bed so perfectly before. My room looked absolutely phenomenal! The Holly Hobby wallpaper that my mother had hung for me was the perfect backdrop for my handmade quilt made by Great Aunt Bessie. My stuffed animals were arranged with purpose and class. My clothes were folded and put away on shelves and in drawers. My feathers and fans were magically placed on my walls, and not a speck of dust was to be found on my dresser. On top of my dresser was my Dookie, spinning happily on his wheel.

"Dookie!" I reached in and grabbed him out. I kissed his furry little face and looked into his black buttony eyes. "I missed you so much!"

"Your room looks fantastic, Holly Hocks!" my mother exclaimed. "Now go get ready for our guests. They have a daughter your same age who goes to your school. Her name is Camellia. They will be here shortly."

I wondered if this was the same Camellia who "knew me." Maybe she really *did* know me.

I was relieved and amazed with being home and in my room. It felt strange at first and I had a sudden pang in my heart for my now forever lost friends, Coriander, Clover, Staniel, and Danley. Would I ever see them again? Were they even real?

Dookie was real. Or was he? Was this real? Were Hickory, Cashew, Juniper, and Ginger real? I got up and put Dookie safely back into his cage. As I was deciding if I should go downstairs, I heard someone coming up. With each step, I heard the unmistakable sound of farts. I started to giggle as I looked out to see my brother, Cashew, climbing his stinky way up the stairs.

He saw me and began to laugh. "Did you hear my bubbles?" he asked.

I bent over with laughter and I knew with all certainty that Cashew and his farts were indeed real.

CHAPTER 49
POST SCRIPT

"Well, I have to hand it to you. Another job well done." Mr. Ree and Major Whoopins congratulated one other as they made their way out of Holly's home and onto the bus.

"That was a close call for sure. Who woulda thought Pankins and the librarian were sisters?" Mr. Ree questioned.

"Ain't no surprise ta me. I kinda saw a resemblance," Major Whoopins said.

"No you didn't! Who are you kiddin'? I'm not one of those gullible kids, man," Mr. Ree jibed.

Major Whoopins laughed. "You right, you right. I had no clue," he confessed.

"Wonder what other secrets are waiting for us when we get back?" Mr. Ree pondered.

"Mr. Mungus and Miss Shapen are secretly married?" Major Whoopins' gut vibrated as he chuckled to himself.

"Mr. and Mrs. Hugh Mungus!" Mr. Ree slapped his knee in hilarity. They continued laughing and ended with a mutual sigh.

"It's gon' be a little while 'fo' we get this one home. We can thank 'bout the possibilities 'long the way."

They looked at Coriander, sound asleep in the rear of the van, as they made their journey back to his home.

"Better buckle up," Major Whoopins ordered.

Mr. Ree turned up the magical music that kept Coriander under the spell.

> *"The Children's Horrible House*
> *The Children's Horrible House*
> *Where you work all day and never, never play …*
> *The Children's Horrible House … ahhh!"*

BE ON THE LOOKOUT FOR:

THE RETURN TO
THE CHILDREN'S HORRIBLE HOUSE

"Hey mom?"

"Yes, Holly?"

"What's your favorite flower?"

"Hmmm..I don't know, I'll have to think about it… What's your favorite?"

"Passionflower."

THE CHILDREN'S HORRIBLE HOUSE

About the Author

N. Jane Quackenbush is a graduate of Palm Beach Atlantic University. She lives in a horrible house filled with mystery and fun in St. Augustine, Florida, a place she finds a lot of material by which she is inspired. A lot of the places mentioned in this book are based on actual haunted buildings, star-filled planetariums and magical gardens deep within The Nation's Oldest City. If you can find and name them, please let Ms. Quackenbush know by contacting her at www.hiddenwolfbooks.com.

You can also stay in touch with N. Jane Quackenbush on Facebook.

N. Jane Quackenbush has also written the following Children's Picture Books:

The Rocket Ship Bed Trip
The Pirate Ship Bed Trip
The Afternoon Moon
and many more in the works!

If you enjoyed reading The Children's Horrible House, please leave a review online.

Watch the trailer on You Tube:
https://youtu.be/hXoZ0XXCyKQ

Made in United States
Orlando, FL
29 October 2024

53236470R00136